Praise for *Fault Lin*

"The pacing is excellent, grabbing readers with danger and excitement right away and keeping the interest throughout. Intriguing and stimulating, *Fault Lines* is the newest must-read."

RT Book Reviews

"Locke combines intense action, credible science fiction, and larger-than-life characters for an enjoyable ride."

Publishers Weekly

Praise for *Recruits*

"Locke's newest novel has everything that readers love. Both intelligent and fast-paced, *Recruits* draws readers in quickly and holds their attention throughout. . . . This is definitely a must-read!"

RT Book Reviews, 4½ stars

"*Recruits* is an accessible, clean science fiction novel ideal for those looking for titles with heart, thoughtfulness, and family values."

Foreword Reviews

Praise for *Renegades*

"Locke weaves multiple exciting narratives, connecting them in unexpected ways, in this fast-paced novel about war, family, and government secrets."

Booklist

Books by Thomas Locke

ENCLAVE

THOMAS LOCKE

Revell

a division of Baker Publishing Group
Grand Rapids, Michigan

© 2018 by T. Davis Bunn

Published by Revell
a division of Baker Publishing Group
PO Box 6287, Grand Rapids, MI 49516-6287
www.revellbooks.com

Printed in the United States of America

Library of Congress Cataloging-in-Publication Data
Names: Locke, Thomas, 1952– author.
Title: Enclave / Thomas Locke.
Description: Grand Rapids, MI : Revell, a division of Baker Publishing Group, [2018]
Identifiers: LCCN 2018020850 | ISBN 9780800727918 (paper)
Subjects: | GSAFD: Christian fiction. | Suspense fiction.
Classification: LCC PS3552.U4718 E53 2018 | DDC 813/.54—dc23
LC record available at https://lccn.loc.gov/2018020850

18   19   20   21   22   23   24   7   6   5   4   3   2   1

The night was beyond black. The windless air condensed the fog into droplets that clung to every surface. Kevin Ritter was on lead. Behind him, twenty-six refugees were strung out in a terror-stricken line. He could hear the panting whispers, he could sense their fear. He had not been out on the line in six months, maybe longer. He had almost forgotten the coppery taste of such dread, or how every minute stretched into hours. Or the weight of every delay.

Kevin flicked on his pocket light, then flashed it again. Both times the mist glowed like weightless jewels. The woman behind him shivered so hard it fractured her breaths. She probably did not even realize she moaned. Her name was Carla, and she was twenty-two, three years younger than he, and very beautiful. Her boyfriend, Pablo, was next in the line. Kevin disliked knowing their names. But they had both introduced themselves, as if the connection were important. Kevin found it best not to forge such bonds with refugees. When he did, they crowded his dreams. But Carla was different. She reminded Kevin of his ex-fiancée. But Kevin's love was lost to him now, and there was nothing he could do about it except yearn for all that would never be.

Carla had confided that they were refugees from Richmond and had fled in order to keep her boyfriend safe. Kevin resisted the urge to tell them to turn around, go home, accept whatever was required to live within Richmond's boundaries. Now they were just another pair of ragged survivors, clutching at the slim hope that Kevin's team could slip them under the wire, fashion the myth of a new ID, and help them forge a new life in Charlotte Township. That was why Kevin risked his life working with the underground railroad. For people like Carla.

Far in the distance a lamp glowed and disappeared, then a second time. Kevin turned to Carla and said, "Wait here for me. Watch for my signal. When you move, keep low and keep silent. Pass it down the line."

"What if you don't make it back?"

She was the kind of woman the bounty hunters preyed on. The militia would eat her alive. Which was probably what fueled her terror. Kevin knew there was nothing he could say that would make it all right. So he said again, "Stay here and stay quiet."

Like the original underground railroad of three centuries earlier, groups of concerned citizens had secretly banded together to help the helpless. Unlike the earlier version, however, Kevin's team did not ship their refugees north. According to rumors, the north was in worse shape than here.

Their one hope was to sneak the survivors *inside*. Fashion new identities. Hide them in plain sight. Doctors became janitors. Engineers turned into carpenters. But there was at least the chance to keep their families together and fed.

Kevin crawled down the gutter on his belly. The wet gravel sawed at his elbows and ribs and knees. A hundred and fifty yards farther on, the electrified border fence had been lifted and bound to the next strand, then replaced with a plastic imitation painted to mimic the rust-streaked steel. He waited a long moment, breathing with his mouth open, listening and scouting. He saw no patrols, so he turned back and waved them forward.

No matter how much they warned the refugees, no matter how sternly the parents spoke to their children, twenty-six untrained people were bound to make a lot of noise. Kevin lifted his head above the gutter's lip and scouted the night. Finally they were crouched behind him, clumped in so tightly he could smell the sweet tea Carla had drunk before leaving their last hiding place. He hissed for silence and listened. Then he aimed his pocket light and flashed twice. Three minutes or an eternity later, the light responded.

"Follow me. Stay close. Pass it down the line." Kevin lifted the fake fence and lashed it into place. He then lowered himself back into the moist grit lining the gully and crawled.

The gutter ran down the west side of the border market, a motley assortment of stalls and taverns. Kevin had not made this trip in two years, not since he had been named co-leader of the local underground. He had followed the example of his father, who had led the railroad until his death, by remaining unseen. His father had been a sheriff's deputy, killed in the line of duty when he stopped highwaymen from robbing a wagonload of refugees. His mother ran the underground now, though only a select few were aware of this fact. Kevin had started serving with the railroad at sixteen.

Their destination was the market's largest vegetable stall, connected on the far wall to a tavern owned by the same proprietor and reputed to have the best food in the border region. Where the two establishments came together, the owner had erected a small warehouse she used for storing both produce and kegs. The rear wall hung slightly over the gutter, as though the owner had overbuilt by error. Kevin slipped under the ledge, turned on his back, and knocked three times.

The warehouse floor came up, a light shone into his face, and a woman hissed, "Who on earth are you?"

"Emergency replacement." Kevin slipped the paper from his pocket and handed it up.

She gave the drawn symbol a careful inspection. "Where's Clem?"

"Broke his leg. You should have received word."

"I did. But you stay alive by staying vigilant." She handed back the paper, uncocked her pistol, and offered him a hand. "So you're the new Clem."

"For this one night."

She watched Kevin emerge, her eyes widening when she saw his size. "Big one, ain't you. You the teacher's boy?"

"Yes." That was how his mother was known, for she taught political history at Charlotte University. "We'll make other arrangements tomorrow. But no one else was available, and the shelter is full to the brim with another group due in."

The stallholder grunted her acceptance and waited as Kevin helped the refugees rise into the hold. The woman told Carla and her boyfriend, "You two, come help me serve food."

She and her volunteers began handing out steaming plates and mugs. It was the first hot meal most refugees had eaten in days.

When all were served, Kevin asked the proprietor, "When do they move out?"

"Soon as they've eaten. You know the destination?"

"Yes."

"Tell me."

Kevin heard the guarded tone and saw the massive six-shooter's handle protruding from her apron belt. Such suspicion became deeply embedded among long-term workers on the underground. They helped the refugees out of principle. Every day refugees like these were robbed, assaulted, murdered. It was against the Charlotte law to help illegals' entry. Over time the dread of capture gnawed at them all.

He replied, "The uptown shelter. By the old stone church."

"Vigilance. That's the key to waking up tomorrow." She waited while the group ate off tin plates filled with her thick, rich stew. "All right, everyone. Gather your belongings and follow me."

Between the tavern and the shop was a narrow alcove used for unloading supplies. A produce truck was parked tail in, the rear flap open, the floorboards removed. The first refugees climbed the wooden steps and balked at what they saw inside.

The woman was ready for this. "You'll be crammed in tight as sardines, but you'll also be safe. No one will ever think there's room down there for anything, much less all you lot. And remember, we'll be halted at least once for inspection.

When you hear the brakes, stop breathing. If an infant so much as whimpers, we're all dead."

After that, the loading went swiftly enough. Packs were used as headrests, and gradually the truck bed became filled with prone bodies, arms clasping the person in front. Kevin remained at the foot of the wooden steps, handing up bundles and infants, urging on the hesitant.

Last in line were the lovely young woman and her boyfriend. At a sign from her, Pablo clambered in first. Carla drew Kevin a step away and said, "You have changes coming. None of them are welcome. All of them are vital."

Kevin felt a sense of electric dread at the words. He realized Carla was one of those known as a special, gifted in some unexplained fashion. He also now understood why the couple had been forced to flee. "Will I survive?"

"You and those you are closest to." The young woman showed Kevin a fathomless gaze. "But only if you heed my call to flee."

That shocked him utterly. "*Your* call?"

She nodded. "When that happens, you must find safety in the company of those called abominations."

Kevin replied, "No one deserves that tag."

"And that is why you must survive." Carla stepped toward the truck. "Be ready for the change when it comes."

Kevin watched her climb up and fit herself in the overtight space. He had a hundred more questions he wanted to ask, a thousand new fears that would ignite his dark hours. But he stayed silent and helped the tavern owner set the floorboards back in place. They tossed empty burlap bags over the scarred surface, retied the canvas backing, and closed the rear gate.

Areas of uptown had been refitted as massive greenhouses to feed the hungry township. The militia troops manning the inner-city checkpoints would scarcely glance at a produce truck making the pre-dawn run.

Kevin stood watching as the truck rumbled off. Then he locked the storeroom's outer door and returned to the secret entry point by the far wall.

He dropped into the gully, carefully resealed the floor panel, and started crawling. He tried not to think about Carla and her strange words. For people like that, there was probably no hope of survival. Even if they did survive, Kevin had no way of knowing where they might land, or how to contact them if he wanted to. Which he most definitely did not.

The sunset was a brilliant Carolina symphony when Caleb stepped from the house. He nodded a greeting to the seven armed clansmen who circled the garden fence. The men were hardshells, a term from the distant past when their forebears populated the western hills, following codes as hard as local granite. The narrow-faced hillsmen were why the enclave had recently voted against permitting so-called abominations to live among them. Sooner or later Caleb's closely guarded secret was going to come out. When it did, he would become just another notch on someone's rifle.

Caleb resembled many of the enclave's young men, tall and strong. He knew some considered him striking, with his tangle of blond hair and the cleft in his chin and his ice-grey eyes. As he approached the two loaded wagons, the smells enveloped him. The stoppered jugs were nestled in fresh straw that held a meadowy fragrance. The rear of each wagon was crammed with victuals and bedrolls and camping gear and Caleb's personal effects. The jugs' contents spiced the air. The first wagon held applejack, the second mostly plum brandy. To Caleb's mind both fruits had been distorted by the distillation, but the fragrance was pleasant enough. There were also a dozen or so jugs of corn whiskey, and Caleb found that smell revolting.

Those jugs and their contents were nothing but a mask.

Eleven months earlier, Dorsey's clan had discovered a vein of gold in their mine. Lucky for the enclave and all their futures, Dorsey led the hill clan that was most trusted, most stable, most capable of understanding the risks that the gold carried. Dorsey's tight-lipped family could also best hold the secret intact. Not just now. For all the years to come.

The region where the Catawba enclave was located, in the Appalachian foothills straddling the North and South Carolina border, had been home to America's earliest gold mines. Back before the Revolutionary War, back before all the violent events that had made and remade their world, the Catawba mines had supplied the gold that was minted into America's first money.

Not a dozen people in the entire state were aware of this, of course. But Marsh, Caleb's father, thrived on such information. He would have taught history at the local community college had he not been so gifted as a trader. Even so, Marsh never lost his passion for learning. Especially about the nation that was now little more than a name and a collection of old myths.

The few people involved all knew the stakes the gold represented. If word ever got out, Charlotte Township would invade, envelop, and put to death their way of life.

Three weeks earlier, Caleb had gone down inside the mine. He and Marsh were the only outsiders granted that privilege. The mine had originally been dug for copper, and the same smelting operation was now used for purifying the gold. The vein itself was a narrow string, scarcely thicker than Caleb's thumb. But the purity was astonishing.

When Caleb had returned to the realm of sky and fresh air, he had seen the feverish glint reflected in the miners' faces. Caleb then understood what his father repeated every time the gold was discussed.

No one could ever know.

The door opened behind him, and his father appeared with two hillsmen. Marsh called over, "How are things, Son?"

"Everything's fine, Pa. The wagons are ready."

Marsh turned to the two bearded men. "Gentlemen, our business is concluded."

Both hillsmen wore the same odd getup—dark jackets and trousers, scuffed high-top boots, and collarless shirts. The younger of the two was Harshaw, leader of the enclave's largest clan. Dorsey's and Harshaw's families had been feuding for generations. A single look at Harshaw's burning gaze was enough to confirm that this man could never know about the wagon's secret treasure.

"I still say we're giving you too much," Harshaw said.

Dorsey replied, "The bargain's been set in place for months now. And it's been agreed on unanimously by the Catawba elders."

"I didn't agree to nothing." Harshaw jutted his chin, which thrust his beard out like a point. Caleb had been watching the man do it for hours and wondered if Harshaw's intention was to make himself as ugly as possible. "The trader Marsh aims on cheating us out of our share."

"That's not possible," Marsh said, his voice mild. Caleb's father was the calmest man he had ever known. Nothing seemed to bother him. Not even serving as trader for the enclave's most contentious hill clans. "The enclave's elders set the commission. I told them whatever they decided would be acceptable."

"Ten percent to the trader, twenty to the enclave," Dorsey said. "The clans discussed it, the elders agreed."

"I still say you're letting the trader rob us of what's rightfully ours."

Dorsey's hand kneaded the grip of his revolver. Caleb could hear the wood squeak softly. "We done covered all this. You can't take it to Charlotte Township yourself. They banished you."

"We'll get another trader. Somebody who ain't claiming more than his share."

"Who else can we trust? There's nigh on thirty silver bars' worth of shine in them wagons. Marsh is the best trader in all Catawba, especially when it comes to getting a good price down Charlotte way."

"We can sell it ourselves round here."

"Anywhere around here we'd be bartering for goods." Dorsey's voice carried a soft burr, a dangerous note of growing impatience. "But Marsh is after bringing us back silver. What does it take to get through that thick skull of yours?"

Harshaw's voice grew hoarse with rage. "You calling me out, Dorsey?"

The entire yard went tense. Caleb could taste the unignited cordite.

Dorsey merely snorted. "Always taking offense and looking for a reason to fight. Which is why you and your clan won't never be traders. The elders made the deal, the clans voted. Marsh's son will take our shine to market."

Harshaw directed his rage at Caleb. "The boy's too young to be handling our wares."

"Didn't you hear nothing we just talked over? Marsh's wife is ill. He can't leave her side. The boy's been trading with his pa since he was old enough to walk. Caleb will get us the best deal going, and he will pay us fair and square. Marsh and his boy have built themselves a good name. Unlike some people round these parts. We can trust them, the deal is the right one, and you know it."

Caleb turned away. The argument faded into the distance as he found himself drawn away by the signal. That was his name for what was happening. He had no idea if there was a better way to describe the experience. He had never spoken of these events with anyone. Not even his father was aware of Caleb's bond with Maddie, though both his parents knew about his other abilities. Five months ago Maddie and her father left for Atlanta, and ever since she had sent him these signals. This was Maddie's gift, not his, and he could not establish a connection unless she first helped him make it happen. Her signal was like a mental knock on the door. All Caleb had to do was open and . . .

But for nine days now, Maddie's signal had only drawn him into silence. She signaled—just a quick contact, almost like she needed to make sure he was there and listening for her—then she withdrew. No explanation, no word, nothing. Caleb had never really missed her until now. Before, he trusted her to be true to their promise. She would go to

Atlanta and settle her father and then meet Caleb in Over-pass. It was the biggest reason Caleb was so eager to depart, so that he could prepare a home for them both. Only now he wasn't sure of anything except that he missed her terribly.

He stepped away from the quarreling men and reached out. His gift was different. But still he tried.

Nothing.

It was when he turned back, his secret sense still on high alert, that he realized what was about to happen.

"*Pa!*"

His shrill tone was enough to jerk all the men about, both the three on the porch and those by the wagons. Caleb pointed a trembling finger at Harshaw. "He aims on murdering you!"

Marsh took a step away, watching his son and Harshaw both. He reached to his belt, then realized his sidearm was still hanging by the front door. "That true, sir?"

"What nonsense is this boy of yours spouting now?"

"I've seen it, Pa! He aims on calling you out, then claiming it was you who turned to violence!"

"I knew there was something wrong with that boy!" It was now Harshaw's finger that trembled as he stabbed the air between them. "He's one of them abominations, and a liar to boot!"

"That's enough." Dorsey stepped between them, his gun in his hand. The metallic click as he cocked the weapon was loud as the gunfire to come. "Keep your hands away from your sidearm, Harshaw. Boys!"

The young men stationed by the wagons cocked their weapons. "We got you covered, Pa!"

"You git on, now," Dorsey ordered, his voice soft. "We're done here."

Harshaw spun on his heel, stomped past Caleb, and strode to where a cousin held the reins to his horse. He jerked the horse around and yelled, "This ain't over!"

Dorsey stood on the porch next to Caleb's father as the two men rode away. "I'll have a word with Harshaw's clansmen. See if we can't put a strong set of reins on that'un."

Marsh offered Dorsey his hand. "Surely appreciate your backing me up there."

"My boys will stay on watch here tonight. I'll be back before daybreak to see you off safe and sound." He nodded to Caleb as he headed out.

Marsh waved Dorsey away, then said, "Son, go say goodbye to your mother."

Caleb jerked away. "What?"

"Harshaw's not a man to let something like this pass." Marsh enfolded him in a fierce embrace. "If you've already left, hopefully we can avoid bloodshed. You best get on down the road. Don't worry about packing. I'll meet you this side of the boundary creek just after daybreak. Hurry now. I don't need your gift to know Harshaw is probably looking for others to back his play."

Kevin stood by the mayor's reception room window, watching four gardeners tend the lawn. Two women knelt and worked on a flower bed while the men held odd-shaped scissors with long wooden handles. They trimmed the border where the grass met the little gully framing the flower beds. The men walked a step, snipped the grass, walked another step, snip. Kevin had never seen anything so perfect in his entire life. Like something from before the Great Crash, he decided, a slow-motion dance to the past. One of the women looked up and met his gaze. She was pretty in a bruised sort of fashion. Then she spotted the badge on his chest and returned her attention to the flowers.

Kevin was a sheriff's deputy, serving the community of Overpass. Officially his region and the much larger Charlotte Township were the closest of allies. For a generation and more, that had been true. But no longer. Charlotte was now ruled by a despot hiding behind the old title of mayor. Silas Fleming was a man with ambitions that reached far beyond his city's current border fences. As a result, the bonds between Charlotte and Overpass were gradually being whittled away.

The doors leading to Fleming's inner sanctum were flanked by two armed militia. The mayor of Atlanta Township had recently offered a reward of ten thousand silver bars to the person who brought him Fleming's head. Six days back, Kevin had apprehended three bounty hunters with forged Charlotte documents and a copy of the wanted poster. On the ride to the mayor's office that morning, the sheriff had assured Kevin they'd been summoned so the mayor could reward him. Kevin hoped with every shred of his being that his boss was right. Every time he thought of the alternative, his chest froze up solid. If the mayor and his militia knew about Kevin helping refugees, he was a dead man.

He spared a silent plea that his mother had received his coded message. As soon as the summons arrived, Kevin had sent a note reminding Abigail not to forget that today was Monday—when, in fact, it was Tuesday. The message meant one thing. Leave everything behind. Don't hesitate. Get to safety. Wait for word.

Kevin realized the sheriff had spoken to him. "Sir?"

Gus Ferguson sat on the leather sofa by the far wall, under a painting of some long-forgotten war. The sheriff was a twenty-year veteran, scarred and grizzled as an old tomcat. "The captain asked you a question."

"Sorry, sir. I was . . ."

Captain Hollis was a man feared throughout the township,

and for good reason. Among the sheriff's deputies, the Charlotte militia was known as the mayor's pack dogs. "How tall are you, boy?"

"Deputy," Gus corrected.

"I'm six five, sir."

Captain Hollis wore the all-black militia uniform, tailored to fit his lean form, and his ironed creases looked like blades. His brown hair was parted along the middle of his skull and plastered down tight as a helmet. He had grey eyes, blank and cold as a lizard's. "You're the one they call Kitten."

All the deputies were given nicknames they referred to as brands. Being branded was part of belonging to the force. But the militia captain turned it into a slur. Even so, there was nothing to be gained from riling the officer. Kevin kept his voice as bland as his features. "That's me, sir."

"Strange tag for a man built like you. What, you ran from a fight?"

"Ritter teaches hand-to-hand combat to our recruits." Gus kept his voice as mild as Kevin's, only an octave lower. "He's called that because he always lands on his feet."

The captain's response was cut off by the double doors opening. A guardsman stepped out and announced, "The mayor will see you now."

███

"Come on in, gentlemen. Make yourselves comfortable." Mayor Silas Fleming remained seated behind his desk, booming a cheery welcome that did not touch his eyes. "I see you've met Hollis, my go-to guy on matters like this."

The desk was built upon a dais raised a foot off the carpeted floor. Only when Kevin was seated did the mayor rise from his chair. Kevin did his best to hide his surprise at how small the man was.

Fleming leaned against the corner of his desk and smoothed wispy hair over his temples. His cuff links sparkled like gold daggers. "How old are you, Kevin?"

Kevin hesitated, then decided the mayor already knew the truth. "I'm twenty-five, sir."

"You lied about your age to enter your father's old force. Allegiance is a fine thing, isn't it, Hollis."

The guards captain lounged in the room's corner, where the shadows melted with his dark uniform. He did not speak.

"Where's your father now, Kevin?"

"Dead, sir. He was killed in the line of duty."

Gus said, "His father was my partner at the time, and my closest friend."

"Now that is a shame. A boy needs his father to keep him on the straight and narrow. He surely does."

Kevin replied, "Sheriff Ferguson has been the best mentor a man could ask for, sir."

"I'm sure he tried, Deputy. I'm sure he tried." The mayor glanced at something on his desk. As he shifted a page around so he could read the script, Kevin noticed the mayor's fingernails were polished.

Fleming went on, "I understand you recently apprehended three armed men dispatched by our enemies to the south. Men intent upon doing me harm. That is highly commendable work, Kevin. Or should I call you Kitten?"

"Whatever you prefer is fine with me, sir."

"See, it's this can-do attitude that made me certain you were the man I needed. You can't imagine how hard it is to find good people these days. It's why I value Hollis like I do. He is the best, absolutely the best there is, at his job. I hope I'll soon be able to say the same about you."

"I hope so too, sir."

"Splendid. Which brings us to the matter at hand. Here I was, planning to reward you for your fine work, when this other item lands on my desk." He used two fingers to lift the paper. "Terrible, this. You know what I have here, Deputy?"

"No, sir."

"It's a death sentence, for not one but two people. Just terrible." He squinted at the page as though studying it for the first time. "I see here we are due to execute a Professor Abigail Ritter and her son. Two upstanding citizens, upright in every way but one."

Time locked up as tight as his chest. Kevin could count the dust motes in the air. He watched the mayor drop the paper to his desk. The light spilled around his minuscule frame. Impossible a man this small could hold such might. The power of life and death. Over him. And his mother.

The sheriff exclaimed, "Deputy Ritter is one of the finest—"

"Gus, we've got the evidence, and we've got the witnesses. The boy and his mother will dangle from two of the township's lampposts at sunrise."

The sheriff protested, "Mayor Fleming, I've served Overpass Township . . ."

The mayor locked gazes until he was certain Kevin's boss was good and silenced. "That's all I'm going to hear from you, Gus. Are we clear?" He turned back to Kevin. "I'm sorry, Deputy. I truly am. But you're guilty, and you're going down."

"Sir, my mother didn't have anything—"

"Don't you even start. It won't do you any good, and it'll

waste my time. And there's nothing I hate more than a time waster."

"Sir, please—"

"You keep on, you're going to get me riled. And you don't want to see that happen. Does he, Hollis."

"No sir. That he does not."

"Hollis here is a specialist at taking care of folks who rile me. It's a dark and painful aspect of this office, needing the services of a man like him. Are we clear?"

"Yes sir."

"I've got to hand it to you. You and your mother ran a tight ship. We've known for some time that an unauthorized conduit for refugees had been at work. Hollis spent far too many hours trying to find the folks in charge. Then a little bird sings in my ear. Not his. Mine. You can't imagine the joy and the sorrow of learning I could finally crush the railroad, but in so doing I would have to end your and your mother's lives."

The words were a hurricane rush in his brain. Entry into the township was officially governed by the mayor's office, but in reality it was controlled by the militia. Everyone who entered Charlotte Township paid in full. One way or the other.

The mayor drew him back with, "Let's get down to business. I have a proposition for you. A get-out-of-jail card. Do this one thing, and you and your mother will be free to go about your lives. The slate wiped clean. Are you hearing me, Kevin?"

He heard himself say, "I'll do anything."

"Of course you will! I liked the look of you as soon as you walked through those doors. I told myself, this boy's got the makings of a survivor. And I was right, wasn't I."

"Absolutely, sir."

"Splendid." He turned his back to the room. "Now tell us everything you know about those folks called specials. Or abominations. Names don't mean nearly so much as what they represent, far as I'm concerned."

Kevin jerked in surprise. Of all the possible avenues of escape he could have imagined, this would not have even registered.

Out of the corner of his eye, he saw Hollis shift forward slightly. The crucial matter was now exposed. This was the strategy of a good interrogator. Control the situation by knowing as much as possible going in, never revealing the precise target. He took a shaky breath. Everything depended upon him getting this exactly right. No hesitations, no signals, no responses except those from a man fueled by raw fear.

He replied, "I've heard the rumors same as everybody, sir."

"You've never brought one into Charlotte Township?"

"Sir, I couldn't say for certain they even exist."

"Oh, they exist, all right. There are too many reports coming in from too many directions for them to be just a myth. Now tell me what you've heard."

"Over the past year or so we've received reports about young people with special talents. Some of the claims are ridiculous."

"Being able to hear people's thoughts," the mayor said. "Ridiculous."

"But some of the others, well . . ."

"Describe them."

"The ability to heal with one touch, we have heard that one a lot."

Hollis scoffed. "Refugees desperate for medical care could have come up with that one."

The mayor glanced over, but all he said was, "Go on, Kevin."

"The power to tell when someone is speaking the truth."

"That would make for an especially damaging opponent at the negotiating table. Wouldn't you agree, Hollis."

Kevin went on, "The ability to turn just about anything into a weapon through thought alone."

The mayor tapped the desk with his knuckles. "And that is *precisely* what interests us here today."

Hollis demanded, "You actually think some kid out there can blow things up with his mind?"

"We'll just have to see, won't we." The mayor rocked up and down on his polished shoes, his hands locked behind his back. "Kevin, last month you attended the gathering of elders from the smaller enclaves south of Washington—what is it called?"

The mayor kept shocking him, both with his knowledge and his changes of direction. "The annual assembly."

"Your mother was supposed to go, wasn't she. But she's taken ill, so you went as her alternate."

"How . . ."

"I hold this office by keeping hold of the township's pulse. Now back to the topic at hand. The matter of these specials came up, didn't it."

"Yes sir. It sure did."

"As a matter of fact, it dominated the entire assembly, especially after it came to light that almost every enclave has confirmed reports of these so-called specials among their numbers. The arguments raged all day and night. I'm given to understand that several august members actually came to blows. Why is that, I wonder."

Kevin swallowed. "A group of elders believes these young people with their special talents are heralds of the Second Coming."

Hollis demanded, "The second coming of what?"

The mayor offered his militia officer a patronizing smile. "Never mind Hollis. He might be uneducated in the finer points of religious thought, but he knows all he needs to. Go on."

"Others talked about how these specials are all the result of illegal experiments. Supposedly the national government started this work just before the Crash." Kevin wiped at the sweat beading his forehead. "There was some kind of secret facility where they changed the genes of human embryos."

"They're not just rumors," Fleming said. "I know because I've had my people in Washington track down the truth. These experiments took place. And now the result is springing up everywhere. Go on, Kevin. Tell us what happened at the vote."

"The elders split right down the middle. Out of seven hundred votes cast, the opponents won by two." That was when the fights had broken out. The losers accused the winners of being more interested in holding on to power than in the safety of future generations. Swift to condemn, exclusionary, blind. Those were some of the words Kevin had heard swirling about the halls. He wiped away his perspiration a second time.

The mayor said, "So the assembly has decided to class these specials as a threat. Why do you suppose that is?"

"My mother thinks . . ."

"Go on, Kevin. Tell us what your mother has to say on the matter."

He saw that the mayor had stopped his heel-to-toe rocking. He knew Fleming was listening intently, even with his back to the room. "The assembly leaders are afraid. They are also resistant to change. They fear the uncertainties these specials represent, especially because their forces are mental. Which means they're also unseen. My mother says the elders fear these specials could threaten their power structure."

"Professor Ritter is a wise and perceptive woman. As are you, Deputy. It's a shame we had to meet under these circumstances." Fleming spun about on one small, polished shoe. "Her analysis is right on the money. But here's something your mother doesn't know. Washington has started rounding up every special they can get their hands on. What happens after that, nobody knows. And a few months back, some of their representatives showed up here. Offering me all sorts of rewards if I'll let them hunt around Charlotte for members of this new breed."

The mayor began pacing between the desk and the window. "Now we've learned our foe to the south, the mayor of Atlanta Township, has started gathering up specials. That is highly confidential, of course. But we have our spies, or rather, Hollis does. Atlanta's mayor wants to set up a secret cadre. Gather together a group of these specials, especially a bunch he's calling forecasters. He wants them to tell him which way to jump." He reached the edge of the dais and flicked a hand in Kevin's direction. "I want you to go out there and find me half a dozen specials. We're going to build ourselves a . . . what was the name we decided on?"

"Task force," Hollis replied.

"The very thing! A special task force. Washington's promised to send us their best hunters very soon now. But there's no telling if they'll let us keep what they find. So before they get started, I want you to round us up a group. Give us a chance to judge these specials for ourselves."

"I'll do my best, sir."

"You'll do more than that! Else I'll have to bring in Hollis. Tell the deputy what will happen then."

The guards captain replied from the shadows, his voice soft and easy and emotionless. "I'll bind you and make you watch as I personally string your mother up from a lamppost. The way I do it, she could last hours. Then I'll end you the same way. The two of you could take all day."

The mayor beamed down at Kevin. "There, you see? Motivation is the key! Now you get out there and show me some results. You and your mother have got yourselves one week."

Caleb spent the night in a tree.

He was utterly miserable but not physically uncomfortable. Zeke, his friend who had built the hide, kept it stocked with a sack of provisions and a clay water jug that still tasted of the shine it had once contained. When the clear night sky drew down an early summer frost, Caleb wrapped himself in old burlap and stayed warm enough. But his desolation robbed him of sleep. The thought that his own stupid mistake had cost him a final night with his family stabbed him repeatedly. If only he had drawn his father away, warned him in secret . . .

In the first grey light of dawn, Caleb ate several handfuls of dried fruit and nuts and drank his fill. Then he heard a soft whistle from below, and a head appeared in the entry. "I figured you'd be here."

"Where's Pa?"

"Trying to calm down the elders." Zeke was Caleb's age but a head shorter. Caleb's best friend possessed a slender, childlike frame and limbs that looked frail as a bird's. His eyes were dark and furtive, his face narrowed into the point of his long nose. The other children called him Rat Boy.

Zeke's father had died when a section of the family mine collapsed. His mother had never recovered and gradually faded away, leaving her only son to fend for himself. He'd gone to live with Dorsey, his uncle, but his five cousins didn't take to this strange little boy invading their already crowded home.

"I know why you did it," Zeke said. "But why did you have to make so much noise?"

"Maddie contacted me. For one instant. I was still . . ." Caleb hung his head. "I'm such a fool."

"No argument there."

"If I could only take back the night."

Zeke shrugged. "It had to come out sooner or later."

Around the time Caleb discovered his new ability, Zeke started bringing in game. The entire enclave talked about his growing ability to hunt. Foxes that had been tearing up henhouses became pelts that Marsh took to market. Venison, quail, pheasant, even wild boar showed up regularly in the butcher's front window. Zeke was never fully accepted, but at least now he was respected. The young man had found a calling. Caleb was the only one who knew how his restless spirit yearned for more.

He and Zeke hunted together, united by secrets they shared with no one else. Caleb's father had seen the boy's need and set up a room for him in the stables. Zeke used it from time to time. But by this point the boy had grown half wild. Or so the rest of the enclave thought. Caleb knew better.

Caleb asked, "Are you still coming with me?"

"Don't talk silly. We been through all this a dozen times. Let it be."

Caleb fumbled with some way to tell him just how much that meant, but all he could manage was, "I'm glad."

Zeke handed over the sack he carried. "Marsh said to give you this."

Inside were a change of clothes, a bar of soap, a razor, a brush, two late winter apples, and a slab of meat in two slices of fresh bread. Caleb's eyes burned anew from knowing that this was his father's way of saying he was still loved, and family. "We best be heading out."

■■■

They mostly held to game trails. They stayed close enough to the road to listen for Caleb's father, then halted by a creek where Caleb washed and shaved. When they reached the meeting point, they slipped into the undergrowth and waited. An hour or so after sunrise Zeke hissed a warning, and a few moments later Caleb heard a wagon wheel squeak.

But as he rose to meet his father, Zeke pulled him back down. Caleb started to swat at Zeke's grip, when he saw how his friend was crouched. Zeke's head was canted to one side, his gaze flickering. Caleb knew that look. He settled back down, tense and ready for trouble.

Two wagons came around a distant curve. His father rode in the lead and Dorsey managed the second. Four saddle horses were tethered to the rear gates. Caleb felt his throat swell up tight. He had no idea what he was going to say to his father.

Then an all-too-familiar voice yelled from the trail leading uphill, "There they be!"

Both wagoners jerked in surprise as Harshaw rode into view. Three strangers emerged from the woods behind him. The clansman called, "Where's your boy, Marsh?"

Caleb's father demanded, "What business is that of yours?"

"We aim on taking him, is what."

Dorsey asked, "Who's this you're riding with, Harshaw?"

"That ain't any of your concern. None of this is."

Dorsey directed his words to the three armed men. "Don't believe I've seen you around these parts before."

"And I'm saying our business ain't with you, Dorsey." Harshaw pointed at Marsh. "It's with the trader's outcast breed."

Marsh cried, "My son is no outcast!"

Dorsey snarled, "You best shut your face if you know what's good for you. We're still inside the Catawba boundary. The elders have had their say and that's the end of it."

"It's my word against yours, where we stand!" The man's dark beard almost hid the glimmer of his teeth. "And I say we're beyond the enclave's markers. Which makes it within our rights to take the boy for the ransom on offer."

Marsh and Dorsey exchanged baffled glances. "What on earth are you going on about now?"

Harshaw used his rifle to jab the air between them. "Atlanta Township's offering good silver for abominations like your boy. Charlotte too, if the rumors are true."

Dorsey turned to the three strangers. "What business is this of yours?"

The oldest of the three had an old knife wound across his forehead, like someone had started to scalp him. Another odd streak of white ran down the center of his beard. "We come after the boy, like he said."

Marsh's voice had grown hoarse with unaccustomed rage. "You're not touching my son."

"We got to go through you, we will." Harshaw leaned over and spit a stream of brown juice into the dust. "Any who get in our way's gonna hang from that oak—"

Harshaw's words were cut off as Zeke leapt straight from the forest to the back of Harshaw's horse.

Zeke moved so fast and silently that he was in place before the men could react. He set a knife to Harshaw's neck and said, "I'm thinking you need yourself a shave."

"Boy, you looking to get yourself killed?"

"I was about to ask you the very same thing." Zeke gripped Harshaw's collar with one hand and kept the knife's blade tight on his neck. "Careful, now. Else you'll want to cause these men to dig you a grave."

When one of the strangers started to draw his gun, Caleb shouted from the undergrowth, "You keep your hands where I can see them."

Marsh yelled, "Caleb? You all right, Son?"

"Sure thing, Pa. I got them covered."

Harshaw snarled at Zeke, "You poke me with that thing, it'll be two graves they'll be digging!"

"Maybe so. But what difference does that make? You been saying for years I'm not worth the air I breathe. Now drop your gun and tell your men to do the same."

The three strangers might have argued, except for the fact that Dorsey and Marsh now had their own weapons out and aimed. Harshaw warned, "You done writ your death sentence, boy."

Zeke poked the blade in deep enough to draw blood. "Tell them. Or die. It's your call."

The man with the white-streaked beard said, "Nobody gets nothing from a shoot-out."

Harshaw cursed and flung his rifle to the crumbling asphalt. "Do what he says!"

"Pistols too," Zeke said. Only when the last gun fell to the earth did he slip off the horse's back. "Nice doing business with you."

Dorsey stood on the wagon seat, his gun steady on the disarmed men. "I believe it's time you headed on back to wherever you came from."

"The elders are gonna be hearing about this!" Harshaw sawed at the reins so hard his horse reared. He yelled at Zeke, "Catawba enclave ain't your home no more. Don't you *ever* come back."

"Ain't you heard? I haven't had me a home for years."

They waited in silence until the four men disappeared around the first bend. Then Caleb scrambled from the undergrowth. Soon as he appeared, Marsh dropped the reins and leapt to the earth. He rushed over and gripped his son in an embrace so fierce Caleb felt new tears squeezed from his eyes. "Oh, Pa, I'm sorry."

"You're all right. That's the most important thing."

Dorsey's wagon seat creaked as he stared down the empty road. "Harshaw's spent the best part of his life searching for the bullet writ with his name." He climbed down and walked over to Zeke. "Son, how'd you ever learn to move like that?"

Zeke was shaking slightly now from the aftermath of combat. "Just picked it up somewhere, I guess."

"Well, you did good." Dorsey studied his nephew. "Harshaw was right. Best you not come back, not for a good long spell."

Zeke shrugged. "I ain't got a whole lot to come back to."

Dorsey offered his hand. "You ever need anything, you holler. I'll do what I can to see you right."

M arsh thanked Dorsey for his help and sent him on his
way. When the horse's footfalls faded into the distance,
Marsh pulled out his grandfather's pocket watch, checked
the time, and said, "We best be off. The deputies don't like
to be kept waiting."

Caleb rode lead while Marsh and Zeke drove the other
wagon. To the north and east stretched Carolina's largest
lake, almost seventy miles across at its broadest point. Behind him, hills grew and condensed as they marched west,
until the Appalachians formed a forested wall. The Catawba
enclave's main link to the outside world was in the southeast
corner, where the woodlands were split by the Charlotte road.
When he was younger, Caleb had often walked to where cow
pastures and Carolina pines met the crumbling asphalt. He
would stand in the middle of that empty road and dream of all
the adventures awaiting him beyond the enclave's boundaries.

Now there was nothing he wanted so much as to return home.

Always before, Caleb had been confident he could handle whatever came. Now he faced the road ahead with doubt and dread.

An hour later, they reached the stream that marked the enclave's outer boundary. Caleb and the others pulled the bits from the horses' mouths and let them drink sparingly. Then one by one they led the wagons across. Concrete stanchions showed where there had once been a bridge. Each year, once the summer rains eased and the harvest was in, volunteers came down to lay fresh stones across the streambed. The Charlotte road was the enclave's main supply route, and these yearly repairs meant heavily laden wagons could cross safely. This late in the year, a number of the stones had been dislodged, and the going was rough. They took turns, riding the reins while the others walked barefoot, holding the bridles.

Once across they unharnessed the horses, then gave them another long drink and half a bag of oats. They gathered by the rear wagon, where Marsh fed them sandwiches and cold tea from the victuals he'd packed. As he handed Zeke his food, he said, "You move faster and quieter than any man I've ever seen. Is that your gift?"

Though the question had been asked in Marsh's habitually mild voice, Zeke tensed up and wouldn't take the food from his hand.

Caleb replied, "Harshaw's not the only one talking about stringing up the specials, Pa."

"Of course. I'm sorry, lad. Forget I asked." Marsh reached over and gripped the boy's arm. "I just want you to know that I'm glad Caleb has you for a friend."

Zeke met Marsh's gaze. "Caleb is the best man I've ever known."

Marsh looked at his son. "You hear that?"

"The way I handled things yesterday . . . it could have gotten us killed." Caleb felt the remorse rise once again. "Now you're going to have all sorts of problems with the elders. All because of me."

"Son, we all make mistakes. Goodness knows I've made more than my share. The questions that make us wise are three: what can I learn, how can I make things right, and where can I improve in the future." Marsh hesitated, then asked, "Does Zeke know . . ."

"About the gold." Caleb nodded, fearing all the mistakes that would come. "It's why I asked him to come."

"In case there's trouble. Good. Because I expect there will be sooner or later."

Caleb wrapped the remnants of his sandwich in the napkin and set it back in the hamper. "This is the farthest I've ever been from home. Right here. I always dreamed about what it would be like, heading out. Now all I see is how I might be the wrong person for folks to be trusting."

Marsh shook his head. "It had to come out sometime, Son. Otherwise you'd never be able to call the Catawba enclave your home. You'd never be able to hide this gift your entire life. Did you consider that?"

Caleb heard the whine of pain in his own voice. "But it didn't need to come out like this!"

"It's bad right now, I'll give you that. But yesterday's confrontation means that Harshaw is your opponent. You know what that signifies?"

Perhaps if he hadn't been so tired he'd have managed

to make heads or tails of his father's words. "Not really. No sir."

"There are bound to be people who are frightened by your gift. People who are tempted to banish the likes of you. But now they'll find themselves allied to the most cantankerous and disliked man in the entire enclave. It won't change the mind of everybody. But it may be enough for some."

Caleb looked at his father. "I'm so scared."

"I have every confidence you will do just fine."

"Come with me. Please."

"We've been through all this a dozen times. Son, even if your mother were well, I'd be staying back. Were I to be there with you, every time you'd negotiate they'd be waiting for me to show up to seal the deal." He fumbled in his jacket and came out with a sealed envelope. "Your mother asked me to give you this. She says you should wait until you're settled to read it."

Caleb probably would have fallen apart had Zeke not chosen that moment to say, "There's somebody coming."

Father and son turned to the east. Marsh said, "I don't hear a thing."

"Three horses," Zeke said. "And they're falling-down tired."

A few minutes later, the three horses plodded wearily into view, their lathered sides declaring they had ridden all night. The man on lead greeted them with a voice gravelly with fatigue. "Sorry we're late."

"Sheriff Ferguson?" Marsh stepped forward. "Where's your deputy?"

"There's been a change of plans." The older man took his time easing from the saddle, then pressed both hands into the small of his back as he straightened. "Hello, Caleb."

"Sheriff."

"Marsh, I need to ask you a favor."

"If it's in my power, I'll be happy to help."

Sheriff Ferguson turned to where the second man was lifting a grey-haired woman off her horse. The woman's features were etched with weary discomfort. The sheriff said, "Hear that? I told you this was the man and the place."

The younger man was both tall and powerfully built. Despite his exhaustion, he studied them each intently from beneath a shock of jet-black hair.

"This is Kevin Ritter and his mother, Abigail. Kevin's been the finest deputy I've ever worked with, save his pa, who died saving my life. Go on, son. Say your piece."

Kevin hesitated, then said, "My ma and me, we've got no place to go."

When he stopped, the sheriff pressed, "Tell them why, Kevin."

But it was the woman who replied, her voice as crisp as a schoolmarm's. "Because that scoundrel of a mayor gave my son an ultimatum. Do the unthinkable or perish. You know the significance of the lampposts outside the mayor's compound?"

"I do," Marsh replied.

"The mayor vowed to string us up unless my son sold out the ones they call specials."

Kevin showed the raw emotion of a man stripped bare by events beyond his control. "Gus and I went straight from the mayor's office to a secret meeting point the Overpass deputies use. Ma was already there. We left with nothing but the clothes on our backs."

"Kevin and his mother have been running the underground railroad around Charlotte," the sheriff said. "Until this happened, Abigail was head of the history department at Charlotte University."

Kevin said, "We'd be grateful if you could grant us a place to stay. I'll do anything, work any job, to earn our keep."

Marsh was about to give his standard response, the one every enclave dweller who traveled beyond their borders learned by rote. How this was not his decision to make.

How the elders voted on every new admittance. How there were dozens who requested asylum for every one granted. How the two would be welcome to stay in the guest cabin and be fed, for three days only, while the council met, the vote was taken, and their fate was decided.

But Caleb broke in before his father could speak. "Pa."

"I . . . Yes, Son?"

Caleb took a breath, then offered Marsh the secret signal they had arranged, "Pa, this is absolutely, extremely important."

Marsh jerked in surprise. Previously Caleb had only spoken those words when a huge trade lay on the line.

When Marsh remained silent, Caleb walked to where the tall young man unsaddled his mount. "What is it you want from us?"

"I already told you. A home."

Sheriff Ferguson interjected, "What is the boy—"

Marsh said, "Give my son a few minutes, Sheriff. Please."

Caleb said, "I mean, what is it you would most like to do?"

The man clearly struggled to focus through his fatigue and his pain. "I never wanted to be anything more than a deputy."

"What was it you most liked about your work?"

Kevin did not need to think that one through. "Patrolling the back roads. Watching the boundary trails. Keeping the folks and the community safe."

That was enough to open the portal. Caleb's own weariness was instantly forgotten. He turned to his father. "Pa, he needs to come with us."

"What, back to Charlotte Township?" Kevin stepped away. "Didn't you hear a word the sheriff just said? The mayor is gunning for us!"

"Caleb's not going to Charlotte," Marsh replied, his eyes steady on his son. "My boy is headed to Overpass. He's setting up a store. The last two times we sold our wares in Charlotte, the militia took more than half in taxes." Overpass was the central market town north of Charlotte and was controlled by the sheriff and his deputies.

"I've heard about that," Gus said. "Protection money, they call it."

Kevin's mother said, "My son won't be able to stay in Overpass forever. Sooner or later Hollis and his dogs will catch wind of this."

The woman's words pushed Caleb deeper into his moment of far-seeing. "Kevin won't remain in Overpass," he replied. "But for a time his presence is essential to keeping us safe."

Marsh demanded, "You sure about this, Son? Absolutely certain?"

"Yes, Pa. I am." He felt a singular sense of bonding with this tired, sad young man. As though standing here and listening to him forged a path not just to safety but to success with his secret quest. He asked, "Why did you turn down the mayor's request?"

The woman cried, "Because I raised him to be a decent human being!"

"Please, ma'am," Marsh said. "Let your son reply."

"I couldn't do what they wanted," Kevin said. "It went against my oath, everything I hold true. I did it to protect . . ."

Caleb nodded slowly. He had it now. The crucial missing component. For the first time since fleeing home, he felt whole. "Us," he finished. "You sacrificed everything you had to protect people like me."

They made camp beside the stream. Abigail walked around a bend in the creek to wash while Kevin gathered firewood. Marsh sent Zeke back for clothes that would fit the former deputy, as he did not want Kevin returning to Overpass in his uniform. While Caleb tended the horses, the sheriff ate a cold meal and talked in low tones with Marsh.

Finally Gus said his farewells, lingering for a few quiet words with his former deputy. Then he climbed into the saddle of a fresh mount, promised Caleb the horse would be waiting for them when they arrived in Overpass, and set off. Kevin stared down the road long after the sheriff was out of sight.

Abruptly fatigue swept over Caleb like a blanket. He found a patch of moss growing beneath an ancient elm and stretched out. The last thing he heard was Marsh asking the deputy and his mother to join him by the fire. Caleb knew his father was trying to take the measure of these two strangers. Upon his return, Marsh would need to convince the elders to let them enter.

Caleb fell asleep to the drone of voices.

···

It seemed as though he was only asleep for a few minutes. Then he awoke to the sound of Maddie screaming his name.

Caleb scrambled to his feet and searched the camp, but all was calm. The sun had not yet reached its zenith, which meant he'd been asleep less than an hour. Zeke was back and stirring a pot set on a cooking stone. Abigail sat on a log talking with Marsh. Clearly no one else had heard anything. But the sense of immense danger did not release him. His heart pounded, his breathing came in tight gasps.

It could only mean one thing.

Kevin walked around a bend in the creek, his hair still dripping wet from bathing. He was dressed in standard enclave garb now—dark trousers held up by suspenders, a collarless homespun shirt with cotton knots for buttons.

Caleb's father smiled his approval and said, "It'll take a hard look to recognize you as once being a deputy."

The words were meant as a compliment, but the young man winced as though he had been struck.

Marsh pretended not to see Kevin's response. He turned to Caleb and said, "You're up. Good. Lunch is ready."

Their meal was a simple one-pot trail stew. There were not enough plates, so Caleb shared with Zeke and Kevin with his mother. Between bites, Marsh continued to ask Abigail about her work as a history teacher and leader of the underground. Caleb tried to pay attention. But with each passing moment, his worries mounted.

He heard Abigail say, "The economic depression that gripped our nation almost a century ago spiraled downward in a series of catastrophic waves. We now know this as the Great Crash, but few people have any idea what that truly means. They look around and see shadows of the past, but without any understanding of who we once were and what we should be aspiring to retrieve."

Marsh replied mildly, "Hard for people to dream about tomorrow when they're struggling to survive today."

"That works perfectly well as an excuse, one I've heard all too often in my classroom," she replied crisply. "But it doesn't change a thing. We have lost sight of our greatness. We have plunged into a new dark age without any idea of what that actually means. Our only hope, our one possibility of lifting ourselves free of this tragic time, lies in remembering the best of who we once were and striving to regain what we have now lost."

Marsh set a battered coffeepot on the stones lining the fire. Caleb gathered up the plates and walked to the edge of the stream. As he scrubbed them with sand, he heard Marsh ask, "What was the best thing about what we've forgotten?"

"The twin visions of democracy and rule of law," she replied without hesitation. "The two go hand in hand. Democracy means government by the people, of the people, for the people. Rule of law means all citizens are held to the same legal standards. Wealth and position change nothing before the law. Now we are so locked in this current age, one dominated by scarcity and violence, that we can't believe things were ever different. We need to wake up once again and resume our quest for greatness as a nation and a people.”

As Caleb returned to the fire, his father said, “I do believe Catawba and our community college will welcome you like the rare gem you are, Professor.”

“Abigail will do me just fine, sir.”

Caleb watched his father pour mugs of coffee and knew he had to talk about Maddie’s silent scream. The thought of revealing yet another component of his secret clenched his stomach tight as a fist. “Pa, there’s something I need to tell you.”

“Should we take a walk?”

“No, the others need to hear. Do you recall Maddie Constance?”

“The young lady you were sweet on.” Marsh smiled. “What a question. Her father is a professor now in Atlanta.”

Abigail said, “Atlanta University used to be a shining light of learning and hope through the entire south. I’ve lectured there on a number of occasions and consider many of the staff close friends. Recently it’s all gone dark.”

Marsh said, “Your mother told me you two were writing. She’s been in touch again?”

Caleb took a hard breath. “We’ve never been *out* of touch, Pa.”

“What are you saying?”

“It started about a year and a half ago. Long before Maddie and her father left. At first I didn’t know what was happening. Now . . .”

Marsh was no longer smiling. “Maddie can read minds?”

“Feelings come easiest to her. And images, like bursts of things she knits together and sends all at once. I can reach out to her, but she has to be listening. It's all her doing." This was proving even harder than Caleb had expected. "We're closer than we've ever been. When she thinks of me and I think of her, we bind together."

His father was as grave as Caleb had ever seen. The dusk and the firelight turned his features cavernous. "Why am I only hearing about this now?"

"Because it's her gift, not mine. And she asked me not to tell anyone. She discovered her gift soon after the elders came out against the specials. Her father, well . . ."

"He was among those who used the term 'abominations,'" Marsh recalled.

Caleb nodded. "Maddie's been taking care of her father ever since her ma died. Her plan was to go down, settle him into his new life, then meet me in Overpass." Caleb felt the sweat dribbling down his spine, plastering his shirt to his skin. "Something's happened in Atlanta, though. About a week ago. It's scared her. A lot."

Abigail shifted forward. "Did she say what?"

"Her last image was about people who'd arrived from Washington." The recollection of her fear pained his heart. "They wore dark suits and had helmets that let them detect people like Maddie. Or at least that's how it seemed. It was the tightest, hardest image she's ever sent me. And since then, all I get are . . ."

"What?" Marsh demanded.

Caleb wiped his face. "Whimpers."

Marsh said, "You should have told me, Son."

"I couldn't, Pa. She made me promise."

Marsh studied his son across the fire. "Tell us about these whimpers."

"Since the Washington folks showed up, I've still been able to reach out and connect with her. But I knew she didn't want me there, so I'd only bond with her for a second. Long enough for her to know I'm there—and worried. Then just now Maddie woke me from my sleep with a scream. Something I've never heard before, and hope I never do again." Caleb felt feverish, sweating and shivering both. "Now she's not there. It's the first time I haven't been able to find her since she discovered her gift. She's gone. And I don't know what to do."

As they prepared for departure, Kevin watched Marsh embrace his son and say, "The enclave knows my worth. They'll soon know yours. You wait. The elders will invite you back."

Caleb started to climb into the wagon, only to be halted by Kevin's mother. Abigail pointed down the empty road leading east. "The people out there want to either condemn you as some especially evil spawn or refashion you into a component of their next power grab. This is *your* talent and *your* life. Hard as it is to look beyond your current distress, I suggest now is the time for you to start deciding what you want to do with your gifts."

Caleb nodded slowly. "That makes sense."

Abigail revealed a rare smile. "Does it, now."

"Yes ma'am. It does. And I'll treat your words as a parting gift."

"That's good, young man," Abigail replied. "For that is how they were intended."

Kevin noticed that Caleb's father stood back a ways with his arms crossed, observing everything. Kevin liked how his mother's words both calmed Caleb and forged a deeper bond with Marsh. He knew any number of such clans—he'd eaten at the table of many, slept in their barns, and managed to save quite a few when they lost everything to the militia's onslaught.

Abigail walked over to where Kevin stood beside the second wagon. "The time for regret is over," she said to him. "You may not indulge this any longer. I forbid it."

Kevin did not know how to respond. His mother was using her classroom voice, loud enough to carry. He sensed she intended all of them to hear and obey.

"Your safety depends upon focusing fully on what lies ahead. Tell me you understand."

"Yes ma'am." He watched as both Marsh and Caleb nodded slow agreement.

"Pay close attention. Heroes of past ages held one quality lost to the mists of time, but vital to your future. They managed to lift themselves beyond the fractured moment and see the bigger picture, the higher purpose." She let that sink in a moment, then continued, "What if everything you have lost, everything you count as error, was in truth meant to prepare you for what lies ahead? What if you were *required* to lose it all in order to gain something far greater?"

Kevin blinked. This was his mother's innate ability, he knew. To rock other people's worlds, shake foundations and assumptions. Grant a new perspective to the old and fearsome and tawdry.

Kevin embraced his mother, slender and strong as a saber. She watched him climb into the wagon seat, then lifted her hand in farewell, a somewhat formal gesture that in the soft grey light seemed proper. "Your father would be so proud of you."

As he gripped the reins, he heard Caleb's father say, "Ma'am, I consider your and your son's arrival to be a gift from above."

...

Kevin took the lead wagon with Caleb guiding the second. Zeke followed on horseback behind. The road ahead was empty except for squirrels and a pair of foxes and a lone wild pig that trotted out of the undergrowth, snorted a challenge, then scuttled away. Weeds and young saplings ate into the highway's edges. Moss covered much of the crumbling asphalt and muffled the hooves and softened the rumbling wheels.

The afternoon shadows began gathering. The wagons creaked and rolled. This portion of the road was so lightly traveled there was little threat from brigands. The township's border was ninety miles ahead, two and a half days' hard ride. Closer to Charlotte Township, especially with the refugees pouring south, they would have to be more careful. Now they rode in silence, Kevin's rifle propped easy on the seat beside him. They made good time.

Toward dusk they entered the region Kevin knew well. The final test all trainees faced was to be given a blank map and assigned an unknown district. They were ordered to make a detailed assessment and report back in a week. Sheriff Ferguson sent the trainees off with the same message he used to address the deputies at every gathering: Survivors survive.

This particular stretch of road had formed the boundary point for Kevin's own test district.

Kevin pulled up in the middle of the road and turned around. "There's an abandoned homestead up ahead with a sweet-water well. We could stop there."

"Sounds good. Zeke?"

Zeke's only response was to rise high in his saddle. He shifted slowly back and forth, moving his entire upper body, like he was sniffing the wind. It was Kevin's first chance to study the guy. Zeke reminded him of the Charlotte gangs. Ferret-faced with a gaze tight and hard. Solitary by nature, and *fast*. In his former position Kevin would probably have brought Zeke in for questioning.

Caleb asked softly, "You got something?"

"Maybe," Zeke replied. It was the first word Kevin had heard him speak.

Zeke leapt down and was gone. Silent and swift as the wind.

Caleb stepped down, stretched his back, then lashed Zeke's reins to the wagon's rear gate. Kevin continued to study the forest where Zeke had disappeared. Caleb said, "He does that."

The trail leading to the homestead was a good deal rougher than the last time Kevin had been up here. There was nothing left of the cabin except crumbling foundations rimming a cellar. The well was an ancient thing, lined in river stone and very deep. There were any number of such abandoned farms, lost to bandits or transformed into fortified inns catering to scallywags. The deputies marked them all.

Kevin retrieved a leather bucket and long rope from their hiding place beneath the cellar overhang. Together he and

Caleb unharnessed the horses. There were seven in all—four pulling the two wagons and three with saddles. The saddle horses served as backup in case of a thrown shoe or lameness. They also signified wealth.

Kevin watched Caleb curry the horses, his features as grim as they were exhausted. Kevin asked, "Still nothing from the woman?"

"No."

"And this has never happened before?"

"No. Even when she's been silent, I could sense her there. Now . . ." He pulled a sack of oats and feed bags from the second wagon. "She screamed and it woke me up. It didn't feel like pain. More like . . ."

"You have that connection with anyone else?"

"I told you. This is all Maddie's doing."

"So you heard her scream, but she wasn't in pain."

"More like she panicked. And then everything went quiet." He gave a visible shudder at the memory, then asked, "What am I supposed to do?"

Kevin gave the answer he thought Gus would have offered. "Gather intelligence. And when you have enough to make a decent plan, you act."

■■■

The shadows were lengthening by the time they'd finished with the horses and set up camp. Zeke still had not returned. Kevin gathered kindling while Caleb foraged. Around the time Kevin had the fire burning, Caleb returned with a double handful of spring tubers, field onions, and wild sage. He washed them in the bucket, pulled the iron pan and sack of victuals from the wagon, and settled down beside Kevin.

Kevin asked, "Where's your pal?"

"Scouting. Zeke will be back."

"You don't mind him skipping out on work?"

Caleb seemed genuinely amused by the question. "First of all, this wasn't work."

"Making camp, then. What do you mean, scouting?"

Caleb pulled a side of smoked pork from the bag, sliced bits into the mix of greens, then set it on a stone to heat. "You'll see."

Their meal had just begun to sizzle when Zeke returned. Kevin considered himself very alert, and still the guy's abrupt appearance startled him. Zeke made *no* sound.

He was shocked even more when Zeke hefted the bucket and drenched the fire. He kept pouring until rivulets of ash streamed around the rim stones. He then poured the remnants into the pan. When there was neither smoke from the fire nor a smell from their meal, he said, "We're being tracked."

Caleb rose to his feet. "Harshaw?"

"Him and the three strangers. And they're armed."

"But Pa took their guns."

"They got more from somewhere."

Kevin asked, "Where are they now?"

"Five miles back, going slow."

"Waiting for dark," Caleb said.

"Did they send out a scout?" Kevin asked.

"No."

Which could only mean one thing, as far as Kevin could see. "They know about this place."

"That's my thinking," Zeke said.

"Who is this Harshaw fellow?"

"Leader of a Catawba hill clan," Caleb replied. "A bad man."

Now it was Kevin's turn to smile. "You really think you know what a bad man is?"

Caleb and Zeke studied him intently. Kevin liked how neither of them felt any need to challenge his words. It drew from him a faintly unwelcome stirring. He was not ready to like them yet.

Zeke took a sack from his shoulder and dumped four quail on the ground. "We can dress these while we decide what to do."

Caleb asked, "What's to decide? We break camp and make tracks."

"Think about what we're facing. Three strangers not from the enclave, hunting us with Harshaw, who wants to string you up."

Kevin said, "Describe the trio."

"Bearded and dirty. One of them has flame-red hair and a cast to his left eye," Zeke said. "The oldest has a scar running across his forehead. And he—"

"Has a streak of white running down the center of his beard that's split by another scar," Kevin finished for him. "The third one is the youngest and is missing two fingers from his left hand. The Greers, father and two sons. Bounty hunters. Hollis uses them for his dirty work."

Caleb said, "I've heard that name, Hollis."

"Captain Hollis is the head of the Charlotte militia." Kevin felt a tightening in his gut. "He has spies among the Overpass deputies."

"So they came looking for you and your ma, then Harshaw told them about Caleb's gift." Zeke nodded. "Makes sense."

"When the mayor confronted me about our work on the railroad, he used the threat to force me to round up . . ."

"Specials," Caleb said.

Kevin nodded. "Zeke is right. We can't move forward with these men on our tail."

"So what do we do?"

Kevin understood now why the hunter had been watching him. "What we have to."

In the fading light of dusk, Zeke led them back to a point where the highway turned sharply to the right. There had once been a second road leading north, but it was now reduced to gravel and weeds. The fork was bordered by a deep culvert where crumbling cement formed a ledge. They could perch out of sight from the road but rise up and have a clear line of sight. They settled into position, then shared a cold meal of dried fruit and a sack of Carolina peanuts and a skin of well water. Soon the earth at their feet was littered with shells.

Kevin said, "As a kid I hated peanuts. Couldn't even stand the smell. Abigail says it's because the winter I turned three, the crops failed and we survived for the entire winter on peanut soup."

"I remember my folks talking about that." Caleb was

seated next to Kevin with Zeke on his other side. "You're twenty-five?"

"That's right. You?"

"Just gone twenty-one. Me and Zeke both. I thought you were older."

"I get that a lot."

"How long have you been a deputy?"

"Eight years. I lied about my age. Abigail convinced Gus to take me on."

"Is that a city thing, calling your mother by her first name?"

"No. It's an Abigail thing."

"Your mother is something. Where's your pa?"

"Dead. Shot in the line of duty. I was nine. The sheriff was his partner. Gus helped raise me."

Caleb started to ask something, then stayed quiet.

Kevin said, "Go ahead, speak your mind."

"It's none of my business. I was just wondering what the sheriff told you before he rode off."

Kevin thought back to the old man's parting words. "He reminded me of the three elements of proper law enforcement. Protect the innocent, uphold the law, and survive."

"Do you have a girl?"

"I did. She broke off our engagement about a year back." He looked around Caleb to where Zeke crouched with his head canted slightly. Listening. "What is it?"

In response, Zeke rose and slipped away.

Kevin had heard nothing. "How does he *do* that?"

"It's his gift."

"And those quail. Four birds without a snare or bow or gun?"

"I asked him once. He said he catches them napping."

Zeke appeared on the road in front of them. "Here they come."

Kevin hefted his weapons and scrambled from the culvert. He whispered to Caleb, "You know what to do?"

In reply, Caleb lifted the shotgun they'd taken from one of the strangers and cocked both hammers. "I'll be ready."

Kevin and Zeke slipped to opposite sides of the road. Kevin gripped his knife in one hand and a crudely fashioned club in the other. He breathed through his mouth, listening intently. A springtime night surrounded him. A nightjar chuckled, an owl hooted, and the leaves to his left rustled with a passing animal, probably a stoat. A few crickets sang. What little wind there was died off. The loudest sound was the hammering of his heart. The minutes dragged.

Kevin tried to tell himself it was just another takedown. He had been involved in dozens. Hundreds. Only this wasn't an arrest, and he wasn't a deputy. Nothing was the same.

His mind drummed with rising doubts. What was he doing, putting his life in the hands of two young men from a backcountry enclave? And for what? His mother was gone. Had he saved her from the mayor just so she'd be expelled from an enclave that didn't value her, and when he wasn't there to protect her? And what about him sitting here, hiding in the weeds? He was outside the law, and what he was about to do would put him utterly beyond . . .

His mind shot back to the immediate moment when Zeke hissed.

A few breaths, then he heard the soft plod of hooves. They came into view soon after, four on horseback. Which meant they felt safe enough to ride grouped together, no scout walking the trail, no outrider, nobody walking ahead to draw fire.

He heard one man grumble, "You said it was right up here."

"Soon," the man in the lead position said. "Hush your jawing."

"You been saying the old homestead is round the next bend for two hours."

"And now I'm telling you to shut up. I never did meet a man who loved to complain—"

The lead man's comment was cut off when Caleb leapt from the culvert, screamed at the top of his lungs, and shot off the first barrel right in front of the horse's face.

As they'd hoped, all four horses reared.

Zeke did as Kevin had instructed, going for the last man, keeping him from bolting. Kevin started for the senior Greer, then changed course when his son managed to clear his rifle from the saddle holster despite the rearing horse. The rifle was on Greer's opposite side, so Kevin did the only thing he could think of. He slammed the knife into the bounty hunter's thigh, all the way down to the hilt. The man screamed as high as a woman. Kevin used the knife to haul Greer out of the saddle. The knife came free as the bounty hunter tumbled to the road. Kevin slammed the club into his skull. Then he spun about, looking for his next target.

It was over.

Two of the riders were down and inert, with Zeke standing over them. The lead rider was the only one still in his saddle. The long streak of white in his beard and the scar across his forehead shone dark in the moonlight. He stared at the shotgun Caleb had jabbed in his gut and said, "It ain't right, threatening a man with his own piece."

"Get down," Kevin said. "Slow and easy."

The bounty hunter did as he was ordered. He glared at Kevin. "I know you."

"And I know you," Kevin said. "You're Jack Greer."

Greer shot a stream of tobacco juice at Kevin's boot. "And I'm talking to a dead'un."

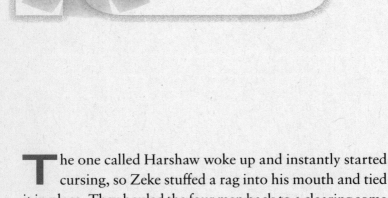

The one called Harshaw woke up and instantly started cursing, so Zeke stuffed a rag into his mouth and tied it in place. They hauled the four men back to a clearing some dozen or so paces off the road, then lashed the four to trees using the Greers' own rope. Kevin sat on a rotting log while Caleb lit a lantern they found in one pack and Zeke tested all the bonds. The older son, the one Kevin had knifed and struck, moaned softly but did not wake up. The other son remained limp, his breathing shallow.

Kevin tried to steel himself against what was coming. But the night's events seemed scripted to him, right down to the revulsion in his gut. He told his new friends, "I know these three. Matter of fact, I arrested them. Twice."

"And both times the militia's sprung us." Old Man Greer

sneered. "What do you think is gonna happen when Hollis hears about this?"

Caleb set the lantern on a stump between them and the captives. "What did you arrest them for?"

"Mostly they prey on refugees. They hunt out the pretty women—the younger, the better. Feed them to the hotels the militia run. Least, they're called hotels."

Old Man Greer wrestled with his bonds. "Boy, you are looking at trouble you can't even . . ."

Zeke darted in from beyond the lantern's reach, a swift dancing motion. The old man sagged against his ropes.

Kevin asked, "Did you kill him?"

Zeke moved back far enough to mask his response from the captives. His blade was clean.

But Harshaw did not know this. He started huffing hard against his gag. His eyes looked ready to pop right out of his head. Kevin walked over and squatted down. His knife rested on the man's thigh. "I'm going to give you the same choice I gave the bounty hunter. Nod if you understand me."

When Harshaw jerked his head, Kevin cut the tie and pulled the rag from his mouth. Harshaw coughed and drew a few hard breaths, then gasped, "You done killed that man!"

From behind him, Caleb demanded, "What were you planning on doing to me?"

"Hey, boy. I didn't mean nothing by that!" His face was greasy-slick in the lantern light. "Come on now, cut me . . ."

Kevin held the blade directly before his eyes. "I ask, you answer. That's how it's going to be. Now tell me how you hooked up with the Greers."

"I seen them around. I used to cart shine into the township. But . . ."

Caleb finished, "He got drunk on his own product, started a fight, spent a month in the lockup, and was banished from Charlotte and Overpass both."

Kevin wondered if he'd come across the man before. "Go on."

"They came looking for me. Said there was a bounty on you and your ma."

"How much?"

"A hundred silver bars."

Kevin rocked back. Caleb said, "What?"

"I didn't believe it either. They showed me the paper. Hundred bars, but only if they brought you in alive. Somebody told them you'd been seen riding off in this direction."

"Just like you suspected," Zeke said.

Now that Harshaw was talking, the words tumbled out. "Me and some of the boys were ready to jump all over that. But Greer said they only wanted me."

When he stopped, Kevin pressed, "Tell us the rest."

"The old man said there was another bounty on the boy. Not him directly. His kind." Harshaw swallowed hard.

"How much?" Zeke asked.

"Fifty silver bars for any what can do like him. I done seen that paper too." Harshaw's neck trembled as he searched out Caleb. His gullet jumped as he forced down a swallow. His voice raised a full octave. "Two quarter shares would set me up for life. It's the only reason I hooked up with them Greers."

Kevin knew it was time to end it. But his knife suddenly weighed a thousand pounds. He could not raise it from his knee. He tried to force himself to act. The strain caused him to pant softly.

Harshaw must have seen his struggle, for his voice rose to a high-pitched whine. "I done answered your questions. Now you got to let me . . ."

Zeke darted in, shockingly swift. The hilt of his knife came down hard on the back of Harshaw's head. His eyes fluttered, then he slumped over. Zeke was already moving toward the two others.

They left the four men lashed to the trees but took their belts and boots and weapons and horses. Kevin assumed it would take the men a day or more to work free. Since they were weakened by the blows, weaponless, and barefoot, there was no telling how long the journey might take them.

They tied the four additional horses to their wagons and headed east. They traveled in silence, the loudest sounds coming from the wagons' creaking wheels and the clop of horses along the broken asphalt trail.

Four hours later, they took the turnoff toward a meadow bordered on three sides by heavy forest. A creek ran along the far end, with several cold fire pits scattered along its length. While they hobbled the horses and let them off to graze, Caleb asked, "What will we do with these extra horses?"

"Tomorrow," Kevin replied, as weary as he'd ever been.

They slept in shifts. When Kevin roused, it was late afternoon and the camp was empty. As he washed and shaved in the creek, Zeke returned to the clearing, dumped a load of fresh kindling, and began building a fire.

Kevin asked, "Where's Caleb?"

Zeke pointed toward the forest. "Off gathering roots. His ma taught him everything she knows, and she knows more than anybody in the enclave. She's been sick for a while now. Caleb's taking it hard."

It was the most Kevin had ever heard the guy speak. "I've never seen anybody move like you do. I'm glad you're on our side."

Zeke kept on breaking twigs and fashioning a tent of the kindling. "You ever killed a man?"

"Twice. Firefights. Used my rifle once, my pistol the other time."

Zeke knelt and blew into the kindling until it finally caught fire. He settled back, his dark gaze on the flames. "I didn't feel anything, striking those men and leaving them like that. I just did what needed doing." He pointed at the quail sectioned and waiting in the pan. "I expect if it came down to killing somebody, I wouldn't feel anything more than when I took the birds."

Kevin recalled sitting with Gus and a couple of the other senior officers after his first shoot-out. The closeness of death had drawn them together in a way he had never known before. "My old boss, he talked about people like you."

"What'd he say?"

"You sure you want to hear?"

"Tell me."

"Gus said they made the best killers. The problem was how to control them, keep them from going dark. He meant—"

"I know what he meant. Did he say how?"

Kevin nodded. The act of remembering his old life was painful. "Partner up with somebody you trust. Someone who's got a solid grip on right and wrong. Accept that you're gifted to be a warrior, and accept the responsibility that your gift brings."

"Your sheriff sounds like a wise man." Zeke slowly fed the fire, then pulled out a coffeepot and filled it from Kevin's bucket. He opened two sacks, ladled in a handful of coffee and half as much sugar. "It's not just this. I watch people in love sometimes. I just don't get it."

"Give it time."

Zeke shrugged and set the pot on the flat stone beside the fire. Caleb returned then, carrying a bundle of herbs. As he washed them in the bucket, Zeke offered, "Caleb's got women everywhere."

"Now that's just a load of old bullwhacky."

"You wait," Zeke said. "We'll show up at that place you said . . ."

"Overpass."

"There'll be this sweet little thing come running up. 'Oh, Caleb, I missed you so. Give me a kiss.'"

"You want to eat your dinner spiced with wet ashes," Caleb said, "you just keep on."

■■■

When they'd finished eating, they broke camp with the ease of three men who'd been traveling together for years. They doubled up the horses tied to the wagon gates, harnessed the others, then pulled down the trail a ways. Kevin went back and swept the camp like he had the clearing. There was no reason he could give for taking such care, but it seemed like the right thing, and the others did not complain.

They rode another fifteen miles and had the road to themselves. The moon cast a silver net over the moss and weeds that flecked the highway's surface, giving it a complimentary sheen. Finally Kevin called a halt and walked back to say, "About five miles ahead, there's an old homestead the scallywags took over. It's been empty since Gus and some deputies drove them off. We should hold up here until daylight."

"Fine by me," Caleb replied. "I never thought I could get so tired just sitting on a wagon and letting horses do the work."

Kevin led them onto a clearing he had used before. They ate a cold meal and Kevin offered to take first watch. But when Caleb was snoring softly, Zeke rose from his bedroll and joined Kevin on the wagon seat. They sat in silence for a time, easy with each other and the night.

Abruptly Zeke tensed and cocked his head. A few minutes passed. Then he relaxed.

Kevin asked, "What was it?"

"Deer."

He had heard nothing. "How far out can you go?"

"Depends."

"Say horses were coming this way."

"Not enough detail," Zeke replied. "Are they shoed, riding hard or ambling along, what terrain. All that matters."

"Four horses that are shoed and saddled," Kevin said.

"Riding the road at an easy pace. If we were back at the camp with the well, would you hear them out on the road?"

Zeke was nothing but a vague silhouette in the starlight. "A lot farther. Especially if they're jawing, like those four were."

"Is it your ears?"

"I . . . Some of it is. But there's . . . I don't know how to describe it. I *sense* things."

"The deputy who taught me trail craft, he spent all his life tracking. Fugitives, feral beasts, it was all the same to him. He once told me the best trackers could taste the wind and say who had tasted it before them."

Zeke shifted around. "Can I meet him?"

"He's gone now." Kevin's memory carried a bitter taint. "Hollis shot him. Claimed it was an accident."

"Did he . . ." Zeke turned back to the night. "Did he feel anything?"

Kevin took his time answering. He knew this absence of guilt really bothered Zeke. He wished his mother was with them. She would have known how to help heal with words. Which pushed him to say, "You remember what Abigail told me before she and Marsh headed out?"

Zeke cocked his head again, only this time it was with the effort of recollection. "About you working toward a higher cause."

"What if the same is true about you? What if you're made the way you are to fulfill a purpose? What if you're made to do what we can't? Because I've got to tell you, I can't imagine a time when a warrior is needed more than now."

Zeke took his time digesting that. Then he said, "I think maybe I'll stretch out for a while."

"Sleep well."

Zeke settled into his bedroll and soon was breathing deep. Kevin returned his attention to the night. For the first time since he'd left Charlotte Township, his heart was not eaten by the acid of bitter regret.

Caleb rose the next morning feeling pinched at both ends. He had not been able to sleep again after his pre-dawn watch. Three times he had reached out, hoping to make contact with Maddie. Her absence gnawed worse than the lack of sleep. As they were loading up, he noticed how Kevin had become a different man. Tighter now. More intent. Exactly as Caleb knew he should be himself.

They returned to the road and set off in the same order as before. Kevin led because he knew the road. Zeke protected their rear. They settled into the journey without discussion. Like they were a unit.

Around midmorning the forest drew back like a veil, revealing a flat expanse of tilled earth and well-tended farms. Most of the structures were set away from the road but within shouting distance of their neighbors. Some were more isolated, and several times Caleb spotted wooden towers holding armed guards.

Gradually the road picked up a bit more traffic. Nothing Caleb saw about the other travelers reassured him. Most were heavily armed. Some of the travelers studied Caleb's wagons with predator gazes. Kevin took to riding with the rifle set across his lap. No one challenged them, though a few looked tempted. Twice Zeke dropped down, tied the horse's reins to the gate of Caleb's wagon, and vanished. The second time, he returned with a small deer draped over his shoulder.

At midday they pulled into an empty clearing set beside yet another desolate farmhouse. Kevin tied the reins around the wagon's brake and walked back. "I know it's early, but this may be our last chance to talk alone. By nightfall there will be others gathering. We've got an hour or so to ourselves. And we need to make some plans."

They built a fire and cooked a meal of fresh tubers and herbs and strips of venison. Kevin noticed Caleb's frown and asked, "Still nothing?"

Caleb realized he meant Maddie. "No."

"Can you, I don't know, call out to her?"

"I've been trying. I'm not even sure . . ." The worry he had been trying to ignore almost swamped him. "I wish I knew what to do."

Kevin gave that a respectful pause, then said, "About eight miles ahead is the outlying farm the deputies have used to hide refugees. If you intend to split your product, now's the time."

"Why would we want to do that?"

"Because if there's trouble with the militia, that way we don't lose everything."

"I thought they didn't operate this far out."

"Usually they don't. I could be worrying over nothing. But if the militia does show up, I'll need to run. And one thing more. If you ever need a hideaway, the farm is a good place to have allies."

Caleb looked at Zeke, who nodded. "Makes sense to me."

Kevin went on, "Give them the extra horses. Ask the chief farmer—his name's Enoch Maskell—to handle their sale and hold your extra produce. Agree to his price. Enoch doesn't dicker."

"You're not coming?"

"I can't. He and almost everybody working there know me from . . . before. If the militia ever found out I'd been back, they'd raze the farm."

Caleb nodded. "Let's do this."

···

They planned while they ate. Kevin took a journal from his pack, tore out a page, and drew the symbol of the fish. He then carefully filled in the Greek symbols, only in reverse, like he was writing in a mirror. He folded the sheet and handed it to Caleb. "Show this to whoever stops you."

Caleb pocketed the paper, rose to his feet, and said, "There's something you need to see."

Kevin glanced at the sky. "Maybe we should hold off—"

"This can't wait." Caleb scrambled under the second wagon and unlatched the hidden cover behind the fore axle. The first of three lockboxes thudded to the earth. He scrambled back out, dragging the case behind him. "Zeke?"

"We're alone."

"Okay." He pulled the key from around his neck and unlocked the box. Inside were lumpish bricks wrapped in burlap and bound in twine. He cut the twine, unwrapped a brick, and held it out. "Trust for trust."

Kevin's eyes were round. "Is that . . ."

"Gold. Go on. Take it."

Gingerly he handled the metal. "How much do you have?"

"A hundred bricks at a quarter-pound apiece. Another sixty waiting for us to set up in Overpass. Back before the Revolutionary War, gold was discovered in the Catawba streams. America's first gold rush was there in our enclave. It ran out almost three hundred years ago, and nowadays most people never knew it happened. Then eleven months ago Zeke's uncle was mining for copper and struck a new vein."

Kevin turned the brick over in his hands. "What is it worth?"

"Near as Pa can figure, about thirty thousand silver bars. But he says we'll be lucky to get half that."

"No one can ever know," Kevin said. "If the mayor or Hollis ever heard about this . . ."

"Don't even talk about it."

Together they slid back underneath the wagon. Kevin helped lift the box and held it in place while Caleb refitted the latches, then rubbed sand over the cover so that it melded with the rest of the wagon's underbelly.

Kevin said, "I hope someday to show you what it means that you'd trust me like this."

Caleb followed him back into the sunlight. He rose to his feet and made a process of dusting himself off. For the first time since waking to the silent scream, he had a reason to hope.

They were a team.

***

The next day dawned hot for May. The air was very still. Dust sparked the air above the road. They descended into a narrow valley that ran north to south, not deep, but still it trapped the heat and left them all panting. When they arrived at the creek meandering along its base, the horses balked at their harnesses. They took the wagons across one at a time, two of them holding the leads by the metal bits and shouting at the horses to move. When they were across and the horses had drunk, they took turns walking down a ways and bathing.

There was traffic now, not steady, but enough to keep them on constant guard. When they dried and dressed in fresh clothes, Caleb and Kevin rode one wagon to a copse of cottonwoods midway up the eastern slope. As they unharnessed the horses, Kevin went through the instructions a final time. Caleb shook his hand, then walked back down the road. Leaving Kevin with the gold.

When Caleb climbed into the wagon seat next to Zeke, he turned and waved up the slope, marveling at how calm he felt about trusting this former stranger.

Kevin's instructions were very precise. Caleb followed them to the letter. He and Zeke took the trail running along the valley's northern ledge, paralleling the creek. It was little more than a game trail, a narrow ledge with two tracks of paler, flattened weeds. Caleb guessed the clan sent out teams once or twice each season to scythe the growth. Even so, he would not want to try this path in a storm.

When they crested the rise, the apple orchard was a mile or so directly ahead of them, just as Kevin had said. The blossoms turned the trees into earthbound clouds.

Midway across the meadow, Caleb reined in and said, "Go ahead and signal."

Zeke stood on the wagon seat, cocked his rifle, and fired off a round.

The report echoed off the trees ahead of them. There was no farmhouse in sight, nor a single living soul. Just the fluffy white cloud of blossoms, beautiful as a myth.

Then someone emerged from the grove. Caleb assumed it was a woman because she wore a skirt. She held the rifle with practiced ease and kept it aimed steady at them as he clicked the horses and rolled forward.

Caleb handed the paper to the woman, just like Kevin had told him to do. She examined it closely, then left, but only after three armed men had emerged from the trees.

Half an hour later, she returned with a tall, lean man. Caleb knew him instantly as a farmer. Though he was probably not out of his thirties, his leathery face was seamed deep as spring furrows. His eyes were tightened into a permanent squint. The hand holding the sheet of paper was broad as a shovel and iron-hard. "Where did you get this?"

Caleb answered as Kevin had instructed. "Abigail Ritter sends her regards."

"She tell you my name?"

"Enoch Maskell."

"Word is the militia captured Abigail."

"They tried. She escaped. Kevin too."

"Where are they now?"

"Safe."

The answer seemed to satisfy the farmer. "The professor told you to seek me out?"

"Kevin said to contact you if I needed help. Which I do. He also said I'd need to pay for your services. Which I can." Caleb hopped down and pulled away the canvas cover. Almost half of their jugs were crammed into the straw. "I want to store this with you."

Enoch walked around to the side and used his teeth to uncork a jug. He sniffed, then smiled. "Plum brandy. That takes me back."

"There are also jugs of applejack and corn whiskey." Caleb gestured to the horses strung out behind the wagon. "We want you to sell the four. Quietly."

The farmer replaced the jug and gave each mount a careful inspection. "These are prime steeds."

Caleb gestured to the pile of weapons. "Sell these too. And the saddles."

The farmer hefted the shotgun and traced a grimy thumb along the name carved into the stock. "This is Old Man Greer's gun."

One of the guards called over, "You took out the bounty hunters?"

The woman turned and hissed. Once. The guard wilted back beneath the trees and vanished.

Enoch asked, "How long do you aim on leaving your stock with me?"

"Few days. Not long."

The farmer rubbed his chin. "Two jugs of the brandy for storing your gear. That'll include feed and stabling for your horses. For the rest, I'll take one horse, one saddle, one rifle, one pistol. My choice."

Caleb resisted the urge to accuse the man of robbery. "Done—if you'll throw in a sack of fresh victuals and another three of oats. We got held up on the road."

"So I see." The farmer set the gun back among the others. "The Greers don't have any friends in these parts. Abigail and her son have friends everywhere. You need help with anything else, you'll be made welcome."

Sunset streaked the western horizon as Caleb and Zeke rode back into the valley. While Zeke watered the horses, Caleb walked the creek bed and gathered edible roots. They climbed the slope to discover the stand of cottonwoods was jammed with people. Even so, the clearing held an air of eerie silence.

Kevin had shifted the wagons over to one side. He waved his rifle in greeting. "How did it go?"

"Fine. Who are these people?"

"I was waiting for you to get back to check them out." He hopped down from the wagon but kept his rifle at the ready. "They've got the look of refugees, but I could be wrong."

Caleb kept his voice low but still feared he was being over-heard. "Why are they so quiet?"

"Refugees get so used to hiding, it's hard to lose the habit.

Especially the kids." Kevin watched Caleb and Zeke untie the burlap sacks lashed to their saddles. "What have you got there?"

"Food for us, including fresh-baked bread. Oats for the horses."

"Sweet. Mind if I share our venison? It could help get our neighbors to talk."

"Fine."

Kevin cut off a chunk large enough to feed the three of them. He lifted the remaining haunches and started toward the other camp. The kids fled at his approach, clearly spooked by his size. Kevin stopped well clear of the fire and waited as two of the men walked over. There were about a dozen adults, perhaps a few more women than men, all of them dark-skinned. In the waning light he could not tell more than that. The Catawba enclave had a number of African American families, a few native Indians, some Hispanics, about two dozen Koreans.

Caleb watched as Kevin handed over the meat and accepted a mug in return. Kevin settled cross-legged onto the earth, but even then he remained outside the group. As he sipped from the mug, he lowered his head slightly and pulled his shoulders inward. The former deputy could not make himself small, but he had experience at adopting as unthreatening a pose as possible.

Zeke rode his horse bareback down to the creek and returned with two buckets of water. Caleb used the last fragments of daylight to gather wood. He started a fire, washed the roots, sliced the meat, and prepared their meal.

Kevin rejoined them and confirmed, "Refugees. They're from the eastern lowlands, a village called Elizabeth. Portsmouth Township took it over. They had to leave."

"Why?" Caleb asked.

"Politics. Two of the women were on the town council. The fat guy there was mayor. The tallest woman is a dentist, the older one there is a nurse's aide. They've applied twice for township passes, Raleigh and Charlotte. But they're twenty-six in all, and they won't split up."

They ate in silence. When the skillet was empty and the coffeepot set on the coals, Kevin said, "They say the militia have set up a roadblock about six miles farther east."

"Is that bad?"

"It's not good. Township militia don't normally operate this far out. This is sheriff's territory."

Zeke said, "They're looking for you."

Kevin carried the look of a warrior. Hard as the gun holstered to his belt. Hard as the night. "Soon as it's dark, I'll slip out and head overland. I'll hold up somewhere to the south. If they set the roadblock where I think it is, the highway jinks hard right about a mile farther on."

"What if it's not you they're after?"

Kevin shrugged. "All I lose is a decent night's sleep. Now listen. A mile or so past that turning, there's a crossroads where three old roads meet. A farmers' market operates there. I'll meet you at the Highwayman's Tavern."

Caleb didn't like them splitting up, but he could think of no argument to stop Kevin. Zeke seemed almost disinterested. He kept searching the night, turning one way and then the other.

Kevin asked, "Anything?"

"There might be patrols. But they're too far away for me to be certain."

Kevin drained his cup. "I better head out." He made a

pack that included his bedroll, their last sack of dried fruit and peanuts, a water skin, an extra knife.

As he strapped on his sidearm, Caleb handed him the second loaf of bread. "Take this."

"I won't say no." He stuffed the loaf on top, shouldered his pack, and said, "See you on the other side."

Caleb watched him stride away. He had no reason to feel as bad about this as he did.

When Kevin had been swallowed by the night, Caleb walked over to the larger camp and introduced himself. "I understand one of you is a dentist."

The woman was taller than him and big-boned, with large, intelligent eyes. "I am, and I'm training another. And a third is a skilled nurse."

"We come from Catawba enclave. We've got two dentists. One is over seventy. The other is despised by just about everybody."

The portly man, the former mayor, said, "We hear most of the farming enclaves don't make outsiders welcome."

Caleb understood what he meant. "If the elders say they are welcome, the enclave obeys. Some folks are better at obeying than others."

The woman declared, "We won't be broken up."

Caleb nodded. It was a familiar refrain. Such times forged strong bonds. "Your profession could make all the difference. Some of our folk have terrible problems with their teeth."

The woman took her time examining him. "Won't you join us?"

It was well past moonrise when Caleb returned to the wagons. Zeke lifted his rifle in a silent greeting. Caleb was exhausted. The day lay on him like a weight. "Can you stay on guard a while longer? I don't think I can keep my eyes open."

"No problem."

He pulled his bedroll from the back, settled it on the earth by the rear wheel, and flung himself down. "Give me an hour."

But the moon had set when he rolled over and sneezed. Zeke was still seated on the front wagon's seat. Only now there was a little girl asleep on the bench beside him. "Her name's Alisha," Zeke said quietly.

Caleb washed his face and poured a mug of treacly thick coffee. "Why didn't you wake me?"

"I'm good." He climbed down, careful not to disturb the little girl. "She had a brother, small like me. The militia took him."

"Which one?"

"She doesn't know. But it wasn't long back, so it was probably Charlotte." He glanced back. "They've been on the road so long she doesn't remember her home anymore. It really bothers her."

Zeke took two long breaths and was asleep. Soon after, the little girl unraveled herself from the blanket, looked sleepily at Caleb, then climbed down and walked back to her family. Caleb watched the slumbering camp, took a walk around the cottonwoods, exchanged a quiet hello with the camp's other guards, then returned to the wagons. And reached out.

The act was so natural now, it was hard for him to recall how shocking it had been in the beginning. The first time Maddie had connected with him, he had felt both frightened and extremely vulnerable. The joining had disconnected him from the reality he had always known, and for a brief instant he saw the world differently—not through Maddie's eyes but rather through her heart. Every time he connected, there was the overlay of her immediate emotions. He knew her fears, her worries, her loneliness, her joy. But beneath this, like a strong current that flowed unseen and yet dominated her life, was her love. For him.

He had grown so accustomed to this, he had forgotten what it meant to be lonely. Now he was cut off from everything he held dear. His family, his home, the enclave. And most of all, from her.

∎∎∎

The next morning, Caleb and Zeke hitched their remaining wagon and were off before the other encampments began stirring. This time Zeke rode in the seat alongside Caleb, his horse tied to the rear gate. As the sun rose above the eastern hills, their wagon crested the rise and passed over an emerald meadow filled with the scent of wildflowers. The road then ran through a break of pines bent and stunted by storms. It seemed to Caleb as though the trees spoke to him. Telling him that the beautiful morning was a myth, that storms were brewing, strong enough to blast him into a new and unwelcome shape.

They left the trees behind, and still the brooding alarm did not retreat. He felt increasingly consumed by a fear he could not even name. Finally he reined in the wagon, stood on the seat, and searched in every direction.

Zeke asked, "What is it?"

"I have no idea." A faint breeze riffled the meadow, streaking the tall grass with silver ripples. Somewhere in the distance a sheep bleated. A pair of crows rose into the sunlight, scripting dark lines in the sky. "Something's wrong."

"Is it Maddie?"

"I don't . . . No. I'm pretty sure it's not her."

"What do we do?"

Caleb reached out, only this time he searched in every direction. It was an unfamiliar gesture. His only connection to what was not immediately in front of him was with Maddie. And she remained silent.

"Caleb?"

He dropped to his seat. "I guess we better go on. Kevin is waiting for us."

Zeke's only response was to ratchet a bullet into the rifle barrel and lay the weapon across his lap.

Four miles later the meadow dropped away, revealing a shallow valley that grew steep farther south. The road swept through a tight double bend, once to descend and once to climb back up, with a ford over a small creek at the base. To the south the creek broadened into a muddy expanse that became a lake during floods. The northern reach was rimmed by barbed-wire fence.

The roadblock was a simple affair, a long wooden arm painted in red and white stripes, with a balancing weight so it could be pushed open and a rope to pull it back down. Two bored militia stood to either side, holding rifles with the muzzles pointed at the earth. Parked just beyond the checkpoint stood an open-sided truck rimmed by padded benches. On the truck's other side was a car. Both the vehicles were painted a glossy black and emblazoned with a shield and two words scripted in gold: *Charlotte Militia.*

Zeke quietly asked, "Is this it?"

"What?"

"The thing that's worried you. Is it the checkpoint?"

"No."

"You're sure?"

"Kind of."

"That's not good enough, Caleb."

"My ability is to find truth in what people say. Sometimes I can move farther out, but always it's based on words somebody has spoken. That's it, Zeke. That's all I know how to do."

Zeke's lean features were furrowed with bone-deep concern. "So what's happening now?"

"I have no idea. This is a totally new thing. All I can tell you is, something is really wrong—"

"Johnny Hayseed!" a man's voice called.

Caleb straightened as a sentry with sergeant's stripes on his black sleeves sauntered over. The sergeant wore a bullwhip coiled to his belt. He was grinning, but there was no humor in his expression or his voice. "Where you boys from?"

"Catawba enclave," Caleb replied as his father had instructed. "Bound for Charlotte Township. My family has been trading with the mayor's combine for years."

"You don't say." He untied the rope holding down one corner of the burlap. He tossed back the coverlet, surveyed the clay jugs, and turned back to the checkpoint. "You want to check this out!"

A tall black woman pushed herself off the truck and started over. Her lean alertness accented the sergeant's corpulent bulk. "What've we got here?"

The sergeant unstoppered a jug and sniffed. "This applejack, boy?"

"Some of it," Caleb said. "The rest is corn whiskey and plum brandy."

The sergeant set the jug back in place. "I believe we'll be satisfied with half your load."

"The proper tariff," Caleb replied, "is ten percent."

"The tariff is what I say it is."

Caleb was not budging. "And if you take it now, I won't be paying another tariff when we pass the township's *real* boundary. So I need a receipt."

The officer's voice filed down to a steel rasp. "You will address me as Sergeant. Or sir."

Caleb felt the day's anxiety coalesce into a burning wrath that seared his throat. "That depends on whether I'm addressing an officer of the militia or a common thief."

The officer's eyes glinted with a piggish rage. "Pull this boy down and lash him to the wheel."

The woman took a step back, disengaging herself. "There are people watching."

Three wagons were pulled up to the checkpoint's other side. A dozen or so travelers milled about as their belongings were dumped out and inspected. All activity had halted now, as everyone watched the unfolding scene.

"Who is gonna bother with what a bunch of refugees say? It's my word against theirs." The fist kneading the whip's handle was scarred and warped. "This boy is going to learn manners."

"I know etiquette," Caleb replied. "And I know a thief when I see one."

"We'll just have to teach you a new tune." He turned slightly and bellowed, "Get over here and lash this boy up!"

The realization of what he'd let himself in for did not fully register until two officers hauled him down.

"The boy who was riding shotgun has gone missing." The woman held to her bored tone. "He took his rifle."

The sergeant whirled about, searched the empty surroundings, then snarled at the watching guardsmen, "You and you. Go find him and bring him back, else I'll lash you up in his place."

The ropes bound Caleb's arms and legs so tight, the wheel hub ground into his chest. He scraped skin off his chin by turning his head. "I'm a lawful trader and I'm filing a protest!"

"You'll soon be protesting a lot louder, believe you me." The sergeant gripped the collar to Caleb's shirt, and in one practiced jerk tore the shirt away. Caleb's back sweated and ached from what he did not yet feel.

The sergeant stepped in close enough for Caleb to see his grin. He unclipped the whip and flipped it out. He twitched the handle, causing it to writhe black and hungry in the dust. "You ready to sing for me?"

A voice hallooed from the opposite rise. "Hey now! What have we got here?"

Well now, will you just get a load of this." Sheriff Gus Ferguson rode a fresh horse and wore a clean uniform only moderately stained by the road. He crossed the creek and eased his way through the cluster of refugees on the checkpoint's other side, all without taking his eyes off the sergeant. "Looks like a lynching to me."

"Go on about your business," the sergeant snarled.

"Yeah, that's what I thought." The sheriff was a broad man, in sound shape for his years. He reined up and eased himself out of the saddle. "This isn't Charlotte Township. And that's the only place your kind are allowed to indiscriminately use the whip."

The sergeant's whip flickered angrily as the sheriff slipped past him. "You touch that boy and I'll *bury* you."

"No you won't." Ferguson unsheathed his knife and asked, "What's your name again, son?"

"Caleb, sir."

"Hold still." He cut the ropes binding his arms, then his legs. Caleb was instantly attacked by a weakness so severe he toppled to the earth. "You all right, Caleb?"

"Yes sir." His teeth chattered so hard he bit off fragments of each word. "Just a little weak is all."

"Climb on up into your rig, now."

The bullwhip coiled and writhed. "Step away from that boy."

A rifle shot echoed down from the eastern slope, and dust exploded by the sergeant's leg. He jerked back so fast he tripped and fell down. Which was good, because the first shot was followed by a second, this one from farther along the hillside. It struck the wagon right beside where the sergeant's head had been.

The sheriff was clearly taken aback by the second shot. He searched the high ground, then turned and surveyed the surroundings. "Where's your other driver, Caleb?"

"H-he took off, sir."

The sergeant scrambled to his feet. "Call off your men!"

"Absolutely, Sergeant. I'll most certainly do that." Ferguson climbed into the saddle and pulled his horse around to where it led the wagon forward. "It'll be my distinct pleasure. Soon as you lot pack up your gear and head on back to where you belong. Let's go, Caleb."

"You can't take us all!"

"Don't need to. All I need to take is you. And I will. Now haul up that barrier or my shooter will plant one in your belly."

▪▪▪

They climbed slowly out of the valley. The sheriff let Caleb and his rig set the pace. Caleb fought down wave after nauseous wave. He didn't feel brave. His residual terror was a stain on the day.

They crested the eastern side and rode through unkempt meadows. As they left the roadblock farther behind, Caleb's sense of distress returned full force. At first he wondered if perhaps it was a rising tide of remorse over yet another foolish deed. But he quickly discounted the notion. Something out there was very wrong.

Ferguson whistled and pointed Caleb toward a grove of ancient oaks. When they pulled up, the sheriff asked, "What got into you back there?"

Caleb climbed down, walked around to the rear of the wagon, and pulled out a fresh shirt. "He was going to take half my goods."

Ferguson's weathered grin exposed a silver tooth. "Man's got you ready for the lash, and all you can think about is your shine."

"Our product could feed the enclave through a bad winter, if need be. And set us up a new source of income for hard times to come."

"Well, you got spunk. I'll give you that."

"Thank you for your help back there, sir."

"Don't mention it." He pointed to where Zeke emerged from the woodlands. "Here's your buddy. And I got a friend out somewheres . . . Here she comes."

The woman rode a dappled grey and carried a rifle across the front of her saddle. "I don't see anyone following."

"Caleb, Zeke, meet Hester Lear."

"Thank you for your shooting, Miss Lear," Caleb said.

"Hester will do." She swiveled her right leg free and dropped to the ground. "And I missed."

Caleb started to thank Zeke, then realized his friend was watching Hester with a stunned expression. The gun dangled from his left hand, forgotten.

Ferguson caught it too and suppressed a grin. "You both did just fine back there."

Hester was a small woman but looked immensely fit. Her skin was honeyed and silky-smooth. Her almond eyes were pushed to a slant by pronounced cheekbones. Her raven hair was cut tight to her head. She was attractive in a dark, feral way. Caleb thought she would probably be both very dangerous and hard to take down.

She asked Zeke, "You fired that second shot?"

He blinked, shook himself, and said weakly, "I missed too."

"Firing at a downward angle will do that."

Caleb asked the woman, "You're a deputy?"

"I used to serve with the Charlotte militia. But I quit."

Ferguson said, "I offered Hester a position as deputy, but apparently she'd prefer to work on her own terms now."

"I have a problem with the militia's brand of authority," she said. "I hate them, and now they hate me. Or at least Hollis does. Kevin helped find me a place among the Overpass private security guards. I owe him. Which is why I'm out here saving your hide."

Caleb pointed along the eastern road. "Kevin said he'd meet us at the Highwayman's Tavern."

"That's about a mile farther on," Hester said. She was a tad shorter than Zeke but still managed to spring into the saddle one-handed. "Let's get moving."

Caleb stopped midway back to the rig. Halted as firmly as if a fist had slammed into him from the sky.

Zeke demanded, "What is it?"

"Something bad has happened."

Zeke moved up beside him. "So it wasn't the checkpoint after all."

"No."

Hester said, "Time's a-wasting, gentlemen."

Zeke glanced over, worried, then turned back. "Can you say where?"

Caleb made a mess of climbing onto the wagon seat. He was still weakened from the close call before. Now his legs threatened to collapse under his own weight. He steadied himself on the hand brake and turned. Searching. "It's something terrible."

Ferguson stepped closer. "What's going on here?"

"Quiet," Zeke snapped. "Caleb, is it Maddie?"

"No!" For the first time, in the first instant, he knew with utter certainty. "It's Kevin."

Hester kneed her horse over close to the wagon. "What are you saying?"

Zeke propped the rifle on the wheel and sprang up beside Caleb. "Where is he?"

"I don't . . ." He finished the circle and started again. He wanted to weep from the dread certainty. "I think he's dead."

Ferguson yelled, "What's going on here, mister?"

Zeke seized Caleb's arm. "Tell me where!"

Caleb followed the shred of sensation, the lurking pain beyond the horizon. He pointed south. "There!"

Kevin pushed on well past moonrise. As he climbed out of the valley he kept flashing on the Charlotte militia patrols he had encountered in his duties. Until that night, he had never fully understood what it meant to be on the run. Exposed, hunted, without the department or his allies or his badge to protect him. If the Charlotte militia caught him, they could do what they liked. He held to a pace one notch below a full run.

The highland meadow was perhaps a mile and a half wide. Kevin passed a couple of long windbreaks of stunted pines. He kept to the high grass until he was well south of the road, then as he turned east he came upon the game trail. His first trainer had called such trails his next best friend, second only to the deputy's own wits. In the moonlight the trail shone like a thin silver ribbon. It curved slightly away from the road, as though the wild animals shared Kevin's fear of the troopers.

The next valley was shallower and the slope clear enough for him to hold to his speed. The creek at its base was a thin sliver of water rimmed by thick mud. He paused long enough to strip off his boots and cram them into his pack. Crossing the small creek proved to be a very hard slog. Kevin sank to knee depth with each step. Pulling one foot free only jammed the other in deeper. The mud clung to him and sucked resentfully with each step. By the time he reached the opposite bank he was gasping hoarsely and sweating despite the night's chill.

The trap was well laid, at the point where the mud ended and the hard earth began. Kevin might have noticed the way cut grass had been laid over the path, had sweat not formed a veil over his vision.

The jaws slammed shut on his shin with a metallic *bang.*

He could not fathom the pain. The metal teeth sank into his leg with the ferocity of a hunting beast. If he'd been told at that moment that the pain alone could kill him, he would have agreed and asked it to happen swiftly. But the agony held him as tight as the trap. And grew steadily worse.

He knew he could not wait. He had to get out before his strength drained away. His leg and foot were black with blood, as was the bank, the chain holding the trap, the water close to where he sprawled. All stained with his rapidly flowing life.

His flailing right hand caught a huge branch, carried downstream by the winter's torrent and now trapped in the muck. He craned and moaned and reached and managed to get both hands around the slippery wood. He dragged it back and fitted it into the trap next to his leg.

Prying the jaws apart was pure unbridled agony.

The pain from the circulation returning to his foot was immense. So too was the exquisite sense of freedom. He shouted against the burning effort required to haul his leg from the metal teeth. He shouted again as he ripped off his shirt and fashioned a tourniquet and wrapped it tight below his knee. Then he lay back, utterly spent.

He knew he was not done. But his mind refused to move beyond the throbbing ache. His gaze was growing steadily dimmer. He knew he had to flee, but he could not move.

Darkness crept in from all sides, silent as feral cats. Kevin did the only thing he could think of, which was to clamber further into the treacly muck. He poured it over himself with the hand not clenching the tourniquet. The mud felt cool and almost welcoming. He lay back, gasped a few final breaths, and was gone.

Kevin's consciousness returned in a few grim flashes, each lanced by pain. The first flash he feared was a mirage. Hester Lear, the former Charlotte militia he had helped settle in Overpass, appeared directly above his head. She called something to people he could not see, then consciousness swam away with the cool creek waters. The second flash was much worse. He woke to a tearing sound combined with a searing, white-hot burst. He screamed, or wanted to, but he only heard a high-pitched whine and had to assume it was his.

"Easy, man, easy." Caleb's face hovered above him. "Zeke has to peel away your trouser and apply a field dressing. We've got to stop the bleeding."

None of the words made sense. Zeke was with Caleb and Hester was in Charlotte. The only item strong enough to defy the pain was his thirst. He tried to ask for water, but he was already gone.

Even so, the next time he rose to awareness, the nozzle of a water skin was fit between his teeth. "Drink, Kevin. That's it—no, easy, slow down, you'll choke."

He drank and coughed and drank and gasped until the effort drained him and the blackness swallowed him whole.

When he next awoke, the world bumped and blurred and he saw everything from a slanted perspective. None of his limbs worked. Then something jostled his leg, and the pain cleared his vision. He realized he was lashed to the hind quarters of a horse, behind the saddle, slumped forward with his arms tied around the rider. The man in the saddle was small and lean and incredibly strong. He grunted with the strain of taking Kevin's weight. The horse's flanks were lathered.

Kevin heard a woman call out, "Time to shift."

"Another mile," the man gasped.

"Zeke, your horse is about done."

"His leg is leaking. The bandage is soaked through. If we don't get him . . ."

Kevin wanted to tell them to slow down, the thumping motion banged his leg. He thought they might like to know his leg didn't hurt so bad anymore. But he did not have the strength to keep his eyelids open, much less shape the words. This time the blackness seemed to welcome him home.

***

Kevin's dreams were tiny shards, so slippery they came and went in sparks of light and pain. Then he awoke, and he was certain of two things. First, that he was truly back.

Second, that he was going to make it. The feeling was so exquisite he sighed noisily.

"Well, well. *Now* you choose to wake. After we have struggled to shift you onto the bed and before I am finished with my work. Which means you are both stubborn and foolish!"

His leg throbbed noisily, but his thirst was stronger. Kevin took that as a good sign. He pried his dry lips apart and whispered his first word in eons. "Water."

"Yes, yes. Of course." The man slipped a glass straw between his lips. As Kevin drank, what he saw registered clearly. The man's black hair was flecked with silver, as was his trimmed beard. His dark eyes were warm and sparked by intelligence and something else—humor perhaps. "Slow, slow, there is no rush. You are safe."

When Kevin sucked out the last drop, the doctor took back the glass and lifted a pitcher. As he did so, Kevin saw his hands and forearms were streaked with blood. When the doctor fitted the straw back into place, he saw the direction of Kevin's gaze and said, "Be glad you had any blood left to stain me with."

He drank until he could not swallow again, then shifted his head and asked, "My friends?"

"Such questions I hear from my patients when they wake. Yesterday I bring a man back from the brink of death and what does he ask? Where is his dog. How I am supposed to know about an animal? But I tell him the beast is fine. He sleeps again. Two hours he sleeps. Because he hears some hairy object is safe." He moved out of Kevin's line of sight. "You, it is friends. This I can answer. Your friends, they are exhausted. The small one, he must be made of iron. Now he is stretched out on my floor. I would think he is dead, but he is snoring. And in all my medical training, never have I heard of a corpse who can snore. At least, not so loudly as this one."

Kevin recalled hearing about a new doctor who had set up shop in Overpass. The man's name escaped him, but he remembered that someone had pointed him out as a genuine curiosity. He had come as part of a group of Orthodox Jewish refugees, driven from somewhere north. The man's heritage was not what made him curious, however. It was the fact that everyone he had treated spoke of him in glowing terms. A doctor who healed, they said. What was more, a doctor who cared.

Kevin doubted the man could recognize him. He had always volunteered for the more dangerous boundary regions, both because he liked the challenge of solitude and because it brought him into contact with the most vulnerable of refugees. People who feared even the relative safety of Overpass. People who would perish if he could not help.

The doctor broke into his thoughts by asking, "Where is your home, young man?"

"Catawba enclave."

"A good enough place by all accounts." He continued to work below the rim of Kevin's vision, tugging gently on his flesh. "I would go there. For my children. But my wife . . ."

Kevin spoke because he sensed it was expected of him. "Catawba is very different from here."

"That I believe. And why is that? Because they grow them big in Catawba! That is the only reason I am working with needle and thread, and not a saw. Because of how they grow you men in Catawba! The muscle of your leg saved your foot, young man. And what muscle there is! Do the Catawba women also grow such muscle?"

"No."

"Of course not. And not all the men either. I knew this already. The small man snoring on my floor is testimony, yes? My teachers would be ashamed of such a question." He tugged and snipped and tugged and snipped. "You are a trader, yes?"

"My friends are. I am . . . a guard."

"A worthy profession in such times as these. The man with your wagon came in earlier. He rode much slower than the little one who snores in my other room. He said to tell you that Gus was helping to settle them in. That is another good man, the sheriff. What is it you bring to sell?"

"Corn whiskey. Brandy."

"So much business you bring me! I should treat you for free. But my wife . . ." He stitched and tugged and snipped again. "And so I remain, and one patient comes in with a head wound. Don't drink the whiskey, I tell him. And if you must drink, don't fight. And if you must fight, bring silver!"

The doctor moved into his vision and glowered. "You and your friends, you have silver, yes?"

"We have applejack."

"Humph. Yes. All right. But don't tell my wife. Now you must turn over. No, no, wait, let me help. Good. Such a mangling that trap gave your leg. Thank goodness you are muscled and not skinny like your snoring friend. Where was I?"

"Silver."

"No, no, no. Business! You really must pay better attention. The man leaves and a woman comes in, she tells me, 'Oh, oh, my liver, like a balloon it is swollen.' I say stop drinking the alcoholic beverage for a month. Eat no fat, no butter, no meat, no salt. Fruit and nut and dark bread only.

Drink nothing but water. She returns a month later. 'Doctor, you're a miracle worker! Look at me, I'm fine!' I say, 'No, your *body* is the worker of miracles.'" He tapped Kevin's thigh with a bloody finger. "Just as *yours* better be, my muscular young friend, if you ever want to walk without a limp."

"I won't lose my leg?"

"Who can say? You must lie and rest. Soon you will walk with the cane I shall give you. After that, who knows what can happen. You could be shot! And then what? You lose more than your leg, that's what! But from this injury, no, I think your leg will stay where it belongs. And so much leg there is here!"

The pain came and went in waves timed to the doctor's needle. But it was bearable now, almost comforting. And this time, when the darkness returned, Kevin greeted it as he would a familiar friend.

Three days after their arrival, Caleb left the shop they had acquired and climbed to the very top of Overpass. The structure stood as a reminder to a time and a world now lost to myth.

A vast north-south road crossed a flat bridge over a deep rain culvert. The bridge was over a half-mile long, a hundred and fifty feet wide, and split down the middle by a crumbling concrete barrier. This was topped by a second bridge, longer than the first, that ran east to west. Overpass was an expanding region surrounding the twin bridges. It had become a melting pot, fed by the constant stream of refugees. The sheriff's department was responsible for law and order, backed up by private guards hired by the Overpass merchants. It was a raucous, bruising place whose frenetic energy was fed by its temporary nature. Most Overpass citizens came from somewhere else and dreamed of someday moving on.

A small park had been established at the center of the top bridge. This had originally been home to a Charlotte militia garrison. But seven months earlier the garrison had mysteriously caught fire and burned to the ground. Volunteers tore down the rubble with the sheriff's tacit approval. Now there was a small lawn and a few swings and a sandbox and picnic tables and trees growing in carefully tended tubs.

Caleb settled on one of the benches facing south and unfolded the letter from his mother. The pages were beginning to fray along the creases, but that hardly mattered, since he knew the words by heart. He read the familiar lines, stowed the letter away, drew a pen and leather-bound journal from his pack, and wrote her back. It was the first diary Caleb had ever kept, and the task of being fully open seemed unnatural. But he was faced with so much that was both alien and hard to fathom, the journaling had become an important part of his very busy days. He had no idea if or when his mother would ever read his words, for the entries were far too sensitive to entrust to the post. But the act of sharing drew her close. Caleb was certain she would approve of his actions.

His mother was an unschooled woman who had always shown a quiet awe at Caleb's voracious appetite for books. She had learned the lore of plants from her own grandmother. Caleb's earliest memories were laced with the odors of potions and elixirs and spices and unguents. The fragrances had formed his home's unique signature, the unspoken welcome that transformed the simple act of opening his front door. He had no interest in the herbal craft. But he had always admired his mother's talent.

Today's journal entry started with news about Kevin. He had lost weight, of course, and looked almost gaunt. But he was already up and moving about the shop with the help of his cane. Pain still robbed Kevin of a full night's sleep, since he refused to drink the doctor's elixir, claiming it left his mind fogged. With his beard and his limp he no longer resembled the deputy he once had been. Now he truly looked the part of a refugee. No one in Overpass gave him a second glance.

The second paragraph was given over to business. In this Caleb was his father's son. Their one-room shop had swiftly gained a reputation for excellent quality and fair prices, and demand for their product remained steady. The previous afternoon, he and Zeke and Hester and two more guards had traveled to Enoch Maskell's farm for the rest of their stock. That new supply was more than halfway sold in just one day of trading.

The third paragraph was harder to write. Caleb's gift was proving invaluable, just as Marsh had predicted. Sometimes he had no idea why he felt drawn in a particular direction, such as when he rented their row house on the lower bridge when they could have doubled their space for half the price by taking a shop at ground level. But what made this portion of the entry hard to write was the personal cost. Caleb felt assaulted by the sheer volume of invisible contacts. People were in and out of the shop all day long. Asking, bargaining, bartering, arguing. He had never known what it meant to be constantly surrounded by the unseen and the unheard. He missed the enclave's solitude and silence.

The fourth and final paragraph took no time at all, for it was the same single sentence he had written every day since their arrival. Of Maddie there was no news. And of the plans he was forming, Caleb would not commit a word of them to paper.

By this point the light had faded to where Caleb could no longer write. He stowed away his pen and journal and gave himself over to reviewing his plans.

The next day he would act.

An hour later, Caleb started back toward their temporary home, as ready as he could be for what was about to begin.

...

As Caleb had hoped, Dorsey and his four sons were waiting for him at their shop. Zeke flitted into view at the top of the stairs, waved a greeting, and returned to the kitchen. Dorsey's hair was still wet from a bath, and his face held the strain from a hard ride.

Caleb greeted them with, "You're a sight for sore eyes."

Dorsey shook his hand without rising from his stool. "The load was ready, and your pa wanted us to make sure you were settling in."

Caleb nodded to Dorsey's sons lining the rear wall. "How is Ma?"

"Marsh says to tell you she's doing better." Dorsey and his sons were simple mountain men, taciturn and fiercely loyal. He slipped three envelopes from his road-worn jacket. "They both send you letters. And there's another from your sister."

"Thank you." Caleb resisted the urge to tear them open and instead slid them under the counter. "I have a long one for you to take back."

"Figured you would." When Zeke descended the stairs

with mugs and the coffeepot, Dorsey nodded his thanks. "You're a good son, Caleb. No matter what folks might say."

"What *are* they saying?"

The oldest boy replied, "Depends on who's talking."

"Marsh is letting them stew for a while. But he aims on using your work here to make a home for all you specials." Dorsey used his mug to include his sons. "Me and the clan are helping him out."

The simple declaration and the iron-hard determination behind it made Caleb's eyes burn. "That means the world."

"Zeke tells us things are going well."

Caleb glanced at the shelves running along the wall behind the counter. They were now restocked with lines of jugs. "If you hadn't shown up, we'd have sold out tomorrow."

"Good thing I came when I did."

"We could use a couple more wagonloads soon as you can deliver them," Kevin called from upstairs.

Dorsey glanced up toward the second-floor landing. "I hear from Marsh you got yourself a new partner."

"Kevin Ritter. Former sheriff's deputy. He was injured in the journey, but he's healing well." Caleb saw Dorsey frown and met the man's worry head-on. "I trust Kevin with my life. And our secret."

Dorsey took a slow sip from his mug. "I don't know as how that was your secret to share."

Caleb sat and waited.

Dorsey glanced at his boys, stolid and silent, a line of black against the rear wall. He then took in the simple store, its worn plank floor, the straight-back stools, and the battered metal trays with glasses and water pitcher and sample jug. The lockbox was kept hidden under the counter, next to a loaded shotgun and pistol. Finally his gaze returned to Caleb. But whatever he was about to say was postponed by Zeke's announcement that their meal was ready.

They ate a one-skillet dinner, steak and vegetables with bread fried in the grease. Coffee with coarse ground sugar for dessert. They ate with good appetite and little talk. When the meal was done, Caleb brought Dorsey and his sons back downstairs.

Dorsey waited while Caleb locked the door and closed the front curtain, then asked, "How are you taking to the big city?"

"I like it all right. But it's not home and it never will be."

"What about Zeke?"

"He's managing the change surprisingly well." Caleb drew out a chair across from Dorsey. "Kevin helps. And Hester. She and Zeke are an item."

"Never thought the boy would settle down."

Caleb said carefully, "I'm not sure you can use the word 'settle' with either of those two."

Dorsey stroked his silver-black beard, the hand seamed and scarred from thirty years in the mine and even longer at the still. "Anybody else know our secret?"

"Just Kevin. I'd like to bring in Hester. She'd help with my plan. But I've been waiting for you to show up."

"The enclave is taking well to Kevin's ma, I'll give you that much." Dorsey offered a rare smile. "That Abigail is one smart gal."

"Her son is a good man, Dorsey. The best."

"Kevin claims you saved his life."

"Zeke was the one who found him, hidden under a layer of mud in a creek bed. Without Zeke—"

"But it was your gift that told the boy where to look."

"That same gift is why I trust him. Kevin and his mother lost everything because they refused to give up people like me and Zeke."

Dorsey nodded slowly. He glanced up to the two men moving about overhead, then asked, "You got your plan worked out?"

"Maybe. That's for you to decide," Caleb replied.

He started by moving behind the counter and unlocking the strongbox. The silver coins and bars made quite a pile. He described the role Hester played in protecting the shop.

Dorsey's sons crowded in, agog at the wealth on display. Dorsey inspected it. "How much is here?"

"What you see. Coins and all, we've taken in just over three hundred silver bars."

He grunted his approval, then said, "Marsh figured on eighty bars for the first load. Ninety, tops."

"We decided to sell straight to the customer," Caleb replied. "But this won't last."

"Why not?"

"The tavern keepers are some of the most powerful people in Overpass. If we keep challenging their status, they'll arrange for us to have an accident. The only reason we've stayed safe this long is because we're dickering with three of them."

"You're just gonna give up control?"

"I planned on doing this from the start. I've showed them the value of our product. I'm making a solid profit. Now I intend to sell a going concern and forge us a strong ally going forward."

"If I didn't know better," Dorsey observed, "I'd say you was scared."

"I'm terrified," Caleb agreed. "It's the only way to survive around here."

Dorsey lowered his voice. "Where's the gold?"

"Hidden under my feet." Caleb stomped on the floor. "Did you bring more?"

"Another sixty bars. The vein is richer than we ever figured was possible."

The news was exactly what Caleb had been hoping to hear. "Which means we have to move now."

Dorsey nodded once. "All right. I'm listening."

Despite the pounding urgency that flooded his entire being, Caleb took the time required to describe the moment he had been bound to his own wagon wheel. He described the refugees who had watched the sergeant uncoil his whip, their belongings scattered over the earth. He talked about the way the refugees had stood there, mute and helpless, as an innocent man was going to be beaten to a bloody pulp.

He then related what it had been like arriving in Overpass, learning that a doctor from someplace called Brooklyn had saved Kevin's life. How they had slept on the doctor's floor for two nights, how the office remained jammed with people and ailments and tales of woe. How over dinner the doctor's wife had described the Jewish family's trek, one that had lasted six months and covered more than five hundred hard miles. To this place. Which the doctor's wife called an answer to a lifetime of prayers.

Caleb stopped then, both to catch his breath and to see if they had questions. Dorsey and his sons glared at the unseen world beyond the locked door, their faces creased and grim.

Dorsey said, "All right. You done scared us awake. Now tell us what you got in mind."

"There is no way I can sell this gold here and be sure of keeping us safe," Caleb replied.

The oldest son started, "But you said—"

"I know what I said. Back inside the enclave it sounded fine and good. But this is a different world, and now I know I was wrong. Sooner or later, no matter how careful I am or how many layers I build in, word is going to get out. The militia will learn the Catawba enclave has a working gold mine. They will rip us out by the roots. They'll destroy everything we hold dear. Our homes will be gone. Our families will join the others drifting down the road, hoping for someplace we can lay our heads and feel safe. Until even a place like Overpass seems like paradise."

Dorsey patted the table softly, gentling his boys before they could speak. "So sell it somewhere else."

"I intend to," Caleb said.

"Here it comes."

"Nashville and Raleigh Townships are out—they're Charlotte's closest allies. Richmond is possible, but we run the risk of the federals hearing."

"Stay away from them government revenuers," Dorsey said.

Caleb took a breath. "Which leaves Atlanta. They are Charlotte's biggest enemy. Even if they heard, they wouldn't talk. For them to get to us, they'd have to go through Charlotte first."

"So it's in their interest to keep things quiet." Dorsey kept patting the polished table. Pondering. "What you need is to make it all the way to Atlanta in one piece."

"With the gold. Right."

"And then find yourself some folks we can trust to keep our secret for us."

"Which is where my gift comes in."

Dorsey's features tightened, and it took Caleb a moment to realize the man was smiling. "So let's hear the rest."

Caleb took his time laying it out, covering his fears and his questions. Through it all, father and sons burned him with their hard, dark gazes.

When he was done, he sat back. Spent and frantic at the same time.

Dorsey nodded slowly, his gaze on his hands. "When Marsh said he was sending you down here on your own, most of the elders feared you were too young. I told them I thought it was the best thing that could happen."

Caleb found himself so overcome by the man's confidence he had difficulty asking, "About Kevin and Hester . . ."

"You do what you think is best." Dorsey kept nodding as he rose to his feet. He offered Caleb his hand. "There ain't another man on earth I'd rather trust with this. And that's exactly what I aim on telling anyone who asks."

They all rose when dawn was little more than a grey tint upon the eastern horizon. They took turns in the washroom and were gathered for an early breakfast when Hester arrived with Sheriff Ferguson. They ate in silence, bid one another luck on the road, and departed. All save Kevin, who was left in solitary control of the shop and its wares.

Caleb, Hester, the sheriff, and Zeke took the Refugee Trail, a well-traveled road that circled west of the Charlotte Township's boundary fence. Midafternoon they reached the main southern highway linking Charlotte to Greenville. There they turned back north again, following the main road. When they arrived at the city's southern transport terminal, the sheriff gathered up their mounts, shook Caleb's and Zeke's hands, gave Hester a fierce embrace, then headed back. Gus Ferguson had no interest in being caught on the Refugee Trail at nightfall, riding alone and leading three good mounts.

They ate a sorry meal at a wayside tavern. As they were finishing their second cup of coffee, a Greyhound bus rumbled up, and they joined a long line of fellow travelers. The bus was a rusted hulk with mud-spattered sides. Even so, Caleb and Zeke approached the vehicle in awe. Hester acted as though it was all part of a day's work. As they climbed aboard and showed the tickets they had purchased in the tavern, their rapt expressions drew smiles from those already seated, many of whom had been first-timers themselves earlier that day. The bus pulled away just as the sun touched the western horizon.

Caleb tried to stay awake and savor the experience of his first ride in a powered vehicle. As a kid he and his friends had raced behind trucks traveling the road between Charlotte and Nashville Townships, begging rides and occasionally leaping onto the rear. Now he was one of the privileged few, seated in a padded chair next to his very own window. Despite the road's rugged condition, they were already moving at twice the speed of a horse-drawn wagon.

The bus rocked and jerked. Once the sun set, there was nothing to see except his own reflection. The window did not open and the overheated air was full of odors. Caleb soon fell asleep.

The next thing he knew, Hester nudged his shoulder and said, "Heads up."

The Greenville Township main bus terminal faced onto a market square, empty that time of night. A cluster of Atlanta militia stood by the bus door as it creaked open. Two of the green-clad troopers climbed on board. "Everybody have your papers ready!"

The first trooper checked ID's, the second collected the fees and handed out seventy-two-hour passes. When Hester showed her badge, the guard demanded, "What's an Overpass guard doing in Greenville?"

"Private hire," she replied, and jerked her thumb at Caleb. "This one's father sent me down. We're three in number. He's got a servant in the back. Zeke!"

He answered as they had agreed. "Ma'am?"

"Move forward and show the officer your papers."

The guard checking Zeke's and Caleb's ID's said, "What do Catawba merchants have for sale down in these parts?"

"Shine," Hester replied. "The good stuff."

Caleb offered, "My pa's sent me to look for a new market."

The guard had heard enough. "Entry fee is a hundred dollars each." He motioned for the next passenger's papers. "Guards and servants cost the same."

For Kevin, once the others left, time became a quarrel-some foe.

When he opened the shop two hours late, a line had already formed outside his door. Word had spread with the night that the shop had received another shipment. Kevin stopped offering drams to the paying customers because there was neither need nor an assistant to help him keep track of who had already plied the battered tin cup. There were a few grumbles at being refused the customary sample. But these quieted when Kevin invited them to come back another day. If there were any jugs left.

Kevin realized he had missed lunch when shadows began ensnaring the road beyond his open doorway. His leg throbbed in a manner that he could only describe as loud. He was about to stop for a much-needed break when the customers halted their friendly banter. A silence settled as swift as a hand closing upon their collective necks.

A brute of a man in a dusty suit and silk foulard stepped through the doorway and smiled in a manner that only heightened the danger in his eyes. "This establishment is closed for the day."

His name was Michael Farrier, and he was known throughout the region as a man not to be crossed. He had been pointed out to Kevin on a number of occasions, but this was the first time they had ever met in person.

Farrier said, "You had to be expecting a visit from me sooner or later."

Kevin tried to match the man's casual nature. "I thought you'd send your muscle to fetch me." The same muscle who stood just inside Kevin's front door. And another out front on the street, telling one and all to go away.

"That would do with most of the folks around here. But you and your lot, you're deserving a different level of attention." Farrier was neither tall nor broad, but his strength was as evident as his latent fury. His smile kept lifting the edges of his beard and crinkling the skin around his eyes. "Would you care to hazard a guess as to why?"

Kevin knew an order when he heard one, no matter how smoothly stated. "You knew we were discussing possible arrangements with two Overpass merchants."

"Without even asking if I'd be willing to offer you a better sort of deal." Farrier played at astonishment. "Did they come with an army, I wondered? Or perhaps some written pass from the authorities to the south? Not that I give a whit what Mayor Silas Fleming thinks, nor his dog Hollis."

Kevin found himself liking the man, which he knew was

as dangerous as trying to pet an asp. Perhaps more so. "How can I help you?"

"Straight to the point. I like that, young man. It shows intelligence, not wanting to waste my time." Farrier chopped the air between them. "Why don't we see just how far this intelligence goes, lad. Tell me why I'm here."

"Our product is the best you've ever tasted. It's robbing your three taverns of business. You want to make sure your competitors don't share in the spoils."

"Now that's the first error you've made," he said. "Michael Farrier has no competitors. None still breathing, that is."

"Other tavern owners, then," Kevin amended. "Strong enough to offer us a deal and keep you at arm's length."

Farrier leaned back in his seat. "Go on."

"You want us to go out of business." Kevin could speak without hesitation because he had spent many dark hours thinking of little else. "You want all the product for yourself."

This time Farrier's smile was broad enough to reveal a gold incisor. "You've given this some thought. Now tell me why you'd be willing to accept my offer."

"Because we want to make Overpass our home," Kevin said. "And because you can protect our future loads from Hollis and his toads."

"Wolves, more like. Hollis and his boyos can't allow you to ply the road unchallenged. Unless I help pave your way. And defang the wolves, as it were."

Kevin waited.

"You've impressed me, young man. And Michael Farrier doesn't impress easy. So tell me where all this is headed."

"You want a partnership," Kevin said. "You offer us protection on the road and sale of all the wares we can produce. Shield us here in Overpass. Give us a place to store what wealth we don't carry back to Catawba. For a thirty percent cut."

"I was thinking more in the order of two-thirds," Farrier said.

"No you weren't."

Farrier inspected him, and for once the genteel veil slipped away, revealing the cunning beast who had clawed his way to the top of the Overpass merchant community. "Half the proceeds, split down the middle, and don't you dare object. Because you know full well I'll be handing over half of a higher price than you'd ever get on your own."

Kevin felt as though he was sticking his good hand through the bars of a lion's cage. "Deal."

■■■

Michael Farrier and his guards departed at sunset. The door to Kevin's shop remained open, but the customers did not return. Only then did the nearness of danger impact him. Kevin knew the potency of such aftershocks. Back when he was working the underground network, the hour after he returned to safety was the hardest. Just like now.

Kevin's leg pained him badly. The prospect of climbing the stairs and making his solitary dinner seemed an insurmountable task. So he sat in the shop and watched the dust motes dance in the warm golden light, and found himself thinking about the woman he had loved and lost.

Louisa had broken off their engagement nine and a half months back. Gradually the pain and loss had diminished, and now he could look back and say that she had been right to depart. Because no matter how much they had loved one another, Kevin was certain he would never have given Louisa what she wanted most.

She sought the good life. She wanted a house with a yard. She wanted a trellis adorned with teacup roses. Pink was her favorite color, but white would do. Two children, a boy and a girl. Two dogs. Dinner parties with children playing in their back garden, while she and her guests laughed by candlelight.

Louisa had loved making such plans with Kevin. He had mostly listened, offering little besides encouragement. She accused him of lacking imagination. In truth, Kevin had admired her ability to ignore the world as it was and color her future with old-fashioned hopes.

As dusk settled and the shadows beyond his doorway lengthened, Kevin recalled how his mother had treated Louisa with the same courteous distance she gave her students. In return, Louisa had confessed to finding Abigail tiresome. Now he assumed his mother had recognized what Kevin and Louisa had both stubbornly refused to accept. That Louisa would do whatever it took to obtain her goals. And Kevin would not.

Arguments with Louisa over his and Abigail's refugee work had grown ever more heated. Louisa had claimed to despise the danger Kevin endured for complete strangers. Finally a tearful and heartbroken Louisa had broken off their engagement, saying that she refused to stay and watch him die.

But as Kevin rose from the stool and limped over to lock the front door, he knew the real reason was something else entirely. Louisa had finally come to realize that he would never, not for an instant, sacrifice his principles to obtain a shred of the luxury she so desperately sought.

What distressed him most of all was also the reason she had come to mind after all this time. He knew there was a very good chance Louisa had betrayed him. He had heard that she had recently become engaged to one of the Charlotte city councillors. The timing was too closely tied to his meeting with Mayor Fleming and Hollis. It was all too easy to imagine Louisa sharing what she knew of his secret nocturnal activities . . .

His bitter musings were interrupted by a tap on the door.

Kevin was midway to the stairs. He turned and shouted, "We're closed!"

The outsider responded with another quiet, rapid tapping.

He limped his way back across the shop, pulled back the bolts, and froze.

A frightened young woman peered up at him. "Please tell me you remember who I am."

Kevin was momentarily frozen by the fact that he had just been thinking about the chain of events that had started with meeting this woman. The reasons why he stood here in Overpass came down to that dark hour, and the realization that his secrets were secret no longer. She showed him the same fear as that night.

"Carla."

"Do you remember what I told you?"

"That I would survive if I fled when I had to."

Only then did she step inside. "That time is now upon us both."

Kevin shut and locked the door. He started to confess how he'd thought that hour had already come, when he and his mother had fled. But he merely asked, "Where is your fiancé?"

"Pablo is with the others."

"What others?"

"It's better if I show you." She watched him limp across the shop and grip the cane leaning by the stairwell. "How have you injured yourself?"

"Long story." Kevin took his time climbing the steps, then entered the kitchen and turned on their cooker. When she followed him upstairs, he asked, "When did you last eat?"

"I don't remember." She remained standing uncertainly in the kitchen doorway. "If you're coming, we must hurry."

"First we'll have dinner and you'll explain why you're here." In truth Kevin assumed he already knew. And though there was little he could probably do to help her, he knew he had to try. He opened the icebox and pulled out everything that was inside. "Now tell me what's going on."

···

Carla and Pablo had met in Richmond. Her father was responsible for the city's power supply. Pablo was from a poor Baltimore family, their city-state firmly within the capital's grip. He had escaped a bad home life through joining the National Guard. Carla was a teacher assigned to the guardsmen's night school. They had fallen in love and confessed their closely guarded secrets, all at the same time.

Kevin did not need to ask what her secret was. "What was Pablo hiding?"

For the moment, Carla ignored his question. "About six months ago, the federal government started hunting specials. My father heard the rumors soon after the round-ups began. His work often took him to Washington, and he saw no benefit in hiding politics from his family. So we learned . . ."

Kevin poured the last of their olive oil into a heated iron skillet, then lay out his four remaining steaks. Two to eat, two more for the road. "Tell me."

Carla had a schoolteacher's ability to adapt the most complex issues into small and understandable portions. She related how the legends were based on fact. In the years leading up to the Great Crash, the federal government had secretly funded genetic research on human embryos. Their aim was to create a new breed of mentally gifted individuals and control their powers.

She surprised him then by asking, "Are you a believing man, Kevin?"

"Hard to say." He took his time chopping vegetables he would grill once the steaks were done. "My mother is. She became involved in the underground movement because of its ties to the early church. For myself . . ."

He turned to face her. Kevin liked how she waited, her hands settled calmly upon the table. Giving him time to inspect himself. "I am bred for action. I'm a doer, not a thinker. For better or worse. I'm happy to let others do the thinking for me. And the believing."

She had a stillness about her that reminded Kevin of his mother. "I hope your wife fills that void in your life."

"I have neither spouse nor fiancée."

"She will soon appear," Carla said.

Her calm certainty rocked him. "Do you know when?"

"First you must survive the coming trial." Her smile was tense but genuine. "As must we all."

He turned back to the stove. "You were saying about the research . . ."

"Some within the church claim the government brought

this upon us. That the Great Crash was caused by defiling the divine will."

He set the steaks on a plate to cool and swept the vegetables into the skillet. "I have no place in such discussions."

"I understand."

Kevin liked that as well, how she felt no need to condemn him for what he was not. "So this research into genetics . . ."

"There is no question that some of the test subjects grew to adulthood. And managed to escape those early containment areas." She spoke with almost a musical cadence. Kevin was fairly certain she was an excellent teacher. "They held to secret identities, which was all too easy in the chaos of those first decades. In time, they became little more than another legend from before the Crash."

Kevin ladled portions onto two plates, set one before Carla, seated himself, and waited while she prayed over their food. As he listened to her soft voice, he reflected on how much like his mother she was.

When she lifted her head, Kevin said, "But what does all this have to do with the here and now?"

She was so famished her hands shook as she cut the meat. She paused for three good bites, complimented his cooking, ate another forkful, then replied, "About six years ago my father started hearing rumors that the federal government had been working on new ways to identify specials. To what end, he had no idea. But then last year, more refugees started to flow in from the north. Families seeking safety from . . ."

"The cull." Kevin recalled hearing his mother use the word. Abigail had no logical explanation for what was happening. She had suspected it came down to a dwindling food supply. But even then, Kevin had his doubts. Food had always been an issue—too many people, barely enough supplies. Having food as a reason for the upsurge in refugees did not explain why it had happened *now*.

Carla went on, "The northern enclaves have always been more closely allied to Washington. They were ordered to make a careful sweep of their populace, hunt down all the specials they could identify, and ship them to the capital." She accepted a slice of bread and held it out for him to ladle on honey. "The most vulnerable had no idea why they were being rounded up. Why their families were being torn apart. All they knew was they had to flee."

"And now they've started hunting specials in Charlotte, and your fiancé got caught up in a sweep." Kevin rose to his feet and discovered his leg had stiffened. He stood in place for a moment, pushing down with his heel, willing the pain to release its hold.

She watched him with grave eyes. "Can you walk?"

"Some. I hope to find us mounts. The question is, what do you expect me to do?"

Carla smiled. "You are to play a crucial role in their escape."

"So there's more than Pablo we're to meet?"

"Yes. About twenty in all."

Which made their successful escape even less likely. "Who are the others?"

"You'll see."

"I can't enter Charlotte."

"You don't need to."

"But you just said they were being held by the militia."

"I could spend all night talking and you still wouldn't understand," Carla replied. "Pablo will manage their escape.

Once that's happened, your help becomes crucial. Now can we please go?"

Kevin had a hundred reasons to refuse. But none of them made any difference. He gestured to the remaining food. "Make us sandwiches for the way while I pack."

...

Carla let him set the pace as they walked to Michael Farrier's tavern. His leg thundered less than he might have expected. Kevin knew it was probably for no other reason than he was excited. Which was an absurd way to feel, given the risks he faced.

The Charlotte mayor had been perfectly clear about the fate that awaited him. His and Carla's capture was almost inevitable. Even so, Kevin was filled with a genuine sense of purpose. This was the life for him, the course he felt destined to take.

When they arrived, he said it was best if he handled this alone. Carla responded, "Horses won't help us if we're not there to meet Pablo on time."

"I'll hurry," he promised, then entered and asked for the proprietor. One of the guards recognized him and led Kevin up the stairs to find Farrier standing by the open front window, grinning down at where Carla stood in the street. "Shame to make a beauty like that one wait, lad. Even for an instant."

Kevin held out the shop keys. "There are five wagonloads of jugs minus one day's sales."

Farrier cast another glance down to where Carla continued to wait. "Where are you off to with the young lovely?"

"We need four mounts, two with saddles, two for supplies," Kevin replied. "Nothing so fancy as to draw the wrong kind of attention. But sturdy and fast. I also need payment for all the wares we have to sell."

"We're partners," Farrier reminded him. "Partners settle up once the goods are sold."

"And the house. I need as much silver as you think it's worth."

Farrier returned to his desk and waved Kevin into a chair. "So it's a loan you're after."

"Only so much as is valued in the house and the goods." Kevin saw Farrier was going to argue, so he added, "In case none of us survive."

"What have you gotten yourself into, lad?"

"The girl downstairs has loved ones being held by Charlotte's militia."

"What makes you think you can help her?"

"There's more," Kevin said. "Caleb and Zeke left this morning, trying to save Caleb's own fiancée from the Atlanta forces."

"Two fools off chasing windmills doesn't mean you should follow their lead." When Kevin did not reply, Farrier added, "Is there a chance I can convince you otherwise?"

"None."

Farrier looked disgusted as he shoved pen and paper across the desk. "Write out in a proper hand, deeding me the shop. And explain to your clan about our partnership."

"You'll give us back the house when we return your money?"

"If you return. And I don't give much credence to your making good on that. But yes, it's yours if you repay me." He waited while Kevin wrote as fast as he could. Farrier inspected the document, initialed the bottom, and sighed in exasperation as he pushed himself from the desk. "Say you're able to free her kin. Where is it you're headed?"

Kevin hesitated, then decided someone needed to know. "I figure on trying to meet up with Caleb down Atlanta way."

"Why are you bothering with them at all?" When Kevin didn't respond, Farrier pressed, "I'm asking on account of how I'm looking for a reason to help you. Even when you're getting yourself involved in such unprofitable nonsense."

"My mother and I, we ran the Overpass side of the underground railroad. This woman and her fiancé were the last two I helped slip into Charlotte."

"And look where that's gotten you." But the fire was gone from him now, and the disdain. "That's a brave thing you and your ma did. Stupid, foolish, and without a hope of seeing a dollar from your troubles. But brave."

"Thank you, Mr. Farrier."

"I'm Michael to my friends." He showed Kevin a ferocious scowl. "Even those I don't reckon on seeing ever again. Now I'll go see to your mounts."

"And the silver," Kevin said. "Please hurry."

The building directly across from the Greenville terminal was a hotel in name only. Caleb, Zeke, and Hester joined the other customers who arrived on the midnight bus. As they waited for a room, Caleb inspected the lobby and decided he would not stable his horse in such a place. Even so, they paid an outrageous sum for two adjoining rooms, then more for dinner to be brought upstairs. They showered while they waited, ate in weary silence, and turned in. He and Zeke both chose to unfurl their bedrolls and sleep on the floor.

Because Marsh was counted among the Catawba elders, Caleb was well versed in regional politics. He knew both Raleigh and Nashville were allied to the vastly more powerful Charlotte. In the same manner, Greenville had thrived by paying tribute to Atlanta. Recently Atlanta had become threatened by Charlotte's increasing interest in the region. Six months back, Greenville officially requested to be joined to its southern neighbor. Rumors abounded over whether they were pushed or made the leap voluntarily.

Atlanta and Charlotte Townships had vied for power ever since the Great Crash. Now they were at each other's throats. The Catawba enclave's elders had repeatedly been warned that it was only a matter of time before the two townships entered an all-out war.

Greenville Township still earned a hefty but precarious income, playing buffer. No bus traveled directly between the two regional fiefdoms. Anyone journeying south changed vehicles in Greenville.

The next morning Caleb, Zeke, and Hester joined other early risers in the hotel diner. After a hasty breakfast, they left the hotel just as the central market was beginning to wake up. They crossed the dusty square beneath a warm summer sun and entered the city's old town.

Greenville had adapted better than many midsized townships, refusing to let the ruined city structures gradually waste away. Instead, they had been torn down and turned into parks and market squares. Caleb and the others crossed two such open spaces before entering a street filled with wealth and elegance. Armed guards were posted at every intersection. Parked along its pristine length were a number of private vehicles. Caleb and Zeke slowed to admire a few, until Hester reminded them that the bus would not wait.

Caleb and Hester entered a stylish men's shop, while Zeke lounged at the front entrance. The sight of all the fancy clothes on display left Caleb not only subdued but questioning his plans. He was on the verge of turning away when a lovely saleswoman walked over, swept a disdainful gaze over his dusty frame, and said, "Can I help you?"

"My guard and I need two sets of clothes," Caleb replied.

"You mean ensembles." Then she realized what he had just said. "Your guard."

"Right. And there's a servant at the front entrance. He'll need shirts and trousers."

She dredged up a far more brilliant smile. "Forgive me, sir, but just to be certain, you can actually pay?"

"In silver," Caleb said.

"In that case, you and your associates are most welcome, I'm sure."

Caleb settled on two pairs of trousers, two open-necked shirts, a jacket, and tooled black boots with a matching belt. He waited while Zeke and Hester were fitted, and frowned his friend to silence when Zeke started to complain over the cost. Caleb paid what was required, and then paid extra for speed. The amount was so staggering he found it hard to maintain his calm mask.

As they were about to enter the palatial bathhouse next door, Caleb was struck by an idea so outrageous he laughed out loud.

Hester demanded, "Something the matter?"

"I need to go back."

Zeke showed real horror. "You're going to spend *more* money?"

"Absolutely. Stay here, I won't be long." Caleb turned away before his friend could argue further.

When he reentered the shop, the saleswoman appeared with lightning speed. "Is there anything else I can do for you?"

Caleb could hardly believe it was he who asked, "Can I hire a private car and driver to take us to Atlanta?"

Kevin and Carla headed south by west, taking the same Refugee Trail used by Caleb and Zeke. A quarter moon rose above tall pines separating them from Charlotte's perimeter wall. Some of the other travelers carried lanterns, which was good, because Kevin had not been this way in over a year. There were more people than he remembered, especially given the hour. These travelers were mostly silent—even the younger children gave off little more than a whimper. They journeyed in every possible manner of conveyance, even some trucks whose innards had been torn out to make way for steam engines. Their belching wheezes were by far the loudest noise.

Carla clearly had a destination in mind, where he assumed they would meet Pablo. For the moment it was enough. They followed other horses riding along the right-hand boundary, hurrying.

Mostly to take his mind off his throbbing leg and the drumbeat of worries, Kevin asked, "What happened before you and Pablo arrived in Charlotte?"

Carla replied in brief snatches, halting whenever other riders moved in close enough to overhear. Life in Richmond sounded fairly good to Kevin's ear, though the couple had lived under the constant threat of Pablo's brigade being called away to the border disputes with Mexico. His company protected the arteries connecting Richmond to the Appalachian townships and the surrounding farms, which were vital to Washington's survival. Carla taught school. Their mothers met and quarreled as mothers do, and planned the wedding. Until the day Pablo brought home rumors of new sweeps. Some new way had been developed by the Washington scientists to uncover specials. What precisely, no one knew. Rumors were rife, none of them pleasant.

Refugees journeying from Washington and townships farther north confirmed the reports. Then Pablo's troop was ordered to set up new barricades along the Washington highways. His company was placed under grim-faced Washington bureaucrats. They erected roadside camps with tall electrified fences topped by barbed wires and guard towers.

Pablo came for Carla and told her what was happening, and they ran.

■■■

The first sign Kevin had of change was a great smear of smoke that drifted over the moon. Then he smelled the camp, a strong mixture of people and animals and grilling meat. They rounded a corner and came upon a large clearing that extended west from the road. People began turning off, searching for an empty spot where they could rest.

Carla slipped from her mount and said quietly, "We leave the road here."

To Kevin's astonishment, she took a narrow trail leading east and north, back toward the perimeter fence. Kevin resisted the urge to tell her how dangerous that was. He sensed it would merely be wasted breath.

The path meandered through a forest of pine and oak before fading entirely away. Somewhere up ahead, Kevin knew, rose the township's outermost boundary wall. He had heard they lined such remote sections of the city's perimeter with traps intended to kill and maim.

Even so, smugglers got through. Overpass was home to families who passed down secret paths to trusted members of each new generation. Kevin suspected the trail they followed was one such route. And yet it vanished up ahead, lost to weeds and a pair of young dogwoods sprouting summer blooms.

He decided he had no choice but to say, "We should turn around."

In reply, Carla lifted her face as though sniffing the night breeze that rattled the branches overhead. Then she lashed her horse's reins to nearby branches and slipped between the young trees and continued on. Kevin hesitated, then followed.

The trail opened up again on the other side, only now it was merely an indentation in the weeds. Carla stepped carefully, and Kevin placed his footsteps directly upon her own. Two hundred paces farther, a guard tower's searchlight flickered over the treetops directly ahead of them. Still Carla continued on. When the tower came into view and the light shone upon armed men patrolling the balcony, Kevin hissed, "We can go no farther."

This time Carla halted. She raised her face once more and shut her eyes. The sweeping light shone upon her clenched fists and taut features. They waited there for what seemed like hours.

Then the searchlight went out.

Shouts rose from the soldiers stationed on the tower as a siren sounded in the distance. The electronic wail rose and fell, spurring the militia to action. Kevin could see their silhouettes as they clattered down the steep stairs. All the lights in this part of the city went out, which made the moon appear brighter still. A second Klaxon began to wail, this one farther away. The soldiers piled into a truck parked beneath the tower, only to discover the engine would not start. Kevin could not make out their words, but the soldiers were clearly frantic. Confused. Angry. An officer shouted above the fray, drawing the dozen or so troops into some semblance of order. They marched away.

Carla whispered, "Here they come."

Kevin found no need to point out that whoever approached would still be on the other side of a triple fence topped with razor wire. Not to mention the possibility of dogs patrolling the no-man's-land between the fences. Or mines and steel traps. Or . . .

Carla pointed. "They're behind that first building."

It appeared this area of Charlotte's perimeter held small factories and warehouses. But there were a good two hundred yards separating the nearest structures from the fence. And another hundred yards of cleared terrain between the fence and the forest. A killing ground, Kevin's combat instructor had called such areas. Bare space stripped of all cover, so that anyone who dared venture across would be decimated by fire from the tower.

Kevin could still see nothing move up ahead. Which was a good thing, because over to his right, high upon the darkened tower, two soldiers still stood guard. He was about to warn her, ask if there was any way for her to halt a suicidal rush by her fiancé, when the impossible happened.

The moon became shielded by a cloud that twenty seconds ago had not existed. A dark mist pushed toward them. The fog grew and extended until it covered the killing ground. Soon nothing inside the perimeter fence was visible. It drifted about the tower's lower supports like a silent tide. If the soldiers up top noticed anything, they did not give any sign. From their perspective, they might have been simply observing a thick ground fog.

Then a head popped from the earth at Kevin's feet.

24

When the last person emerged from the tunnel, Kevin and Carla led them back to where the main road joined the camp. The underground passage had left the group and their packs streaked with mud. The nineteen exhausted newcomers were aged between ten or eleven and midforties. Pablo was in his late twenties, a few years older than Kevin and Carla. There was no question that he served as the group's leader. Anytime Kevin or Carla made a suggestion or directed their path, the newcomers looked to Pablo for confirmation. Whenever he spoke, they moved instantly, tired as they were, without protest or question. They did not merely follow him. They trusted Pablo to see them through.

When they reached the clearing, firelight illuminated a group that looked pretty much like everyone else. Their passage along the camp's perimeter drew little attention. Together Kevin and Carla and Pablo led the group south of the main camp. They crossed a narrow creek that supplied the travelers with fresh water. Beyond that rose a stand of fruit trees, probably apple. The space was relatively empty because the densely packed trees kept out all transport except the odd wheelbarrow. Even getting the horses through the undergrowth proved difficult.

Kevin let the horses drink their fill, then led them to a narrow meadow where the mounts of other travelers had been hobbled and left to graze. The earth surrounding his group's bedding was ribbed with tree roots, but he doubted any of them would be awake long enough to complain. Pablo said he and Kevin and Carla would take first watch, then pointed to others, making sure each person understood who they were to wake and when. One of each group was assigned to watch the horses.

Pablo was quiet and lean, with a middle-weight boxer's taut build. He stood about five ten, almost a head shorter than Kevin. He was very self-contained, very calm even though he shared the others' exhaustion. He reminded Kevin of Zeke but without the lightning speed. He and Carla were clearly in love. Every time they passed one another, they shared a look, a caress, a soft word. Kevin found himself aching for what he had once known.

When the others were bedded down and it was just the three of them, Kevin asked, "You're a special as well as Carla?"

Pablo settled where he could clearly see the horses and replied, "We don't like that term."

"Or abomination," Carla said. "Or perversion."

"Those are all tags other people apply to us," Pablo said.

"So what do you call yourselves?"

"Adepts." Pablo shifted so as to gauge Kevin's response. As though he half expected Kevin to laugh.

Kevin said, "It suits you." As Pablo relaxed slightly, Kevin went on, "So you are one."

"Yes."

"What is your . . ."

"We prefer the term 'specialist skill.' Or 'gift.' We use both." Pablo's smile was as spare as the rest of him, a simple rearranging of his lips and the skin around his eyes. "What I can and can't do needs to wait."

"It's hard to explain?"

"Hard to conceive," Carla corrected. "Best if he shows you."

"When there's time," Pablo said.

Kevin decided he had no trouble with waiting. He liked them both, and liked even more how their concern for these others dominated their lives. "So the lights going out and the truck not starting . . ."

Pablo pointed to one of the larger slumbering forms. "Barry. Electromagnetic wave control."

Kevin stared out over the crew, thinking that such traits as these would not be readily surrendered by Hollis or the mayor. "Are we safe here for the night?"

"They need to rest," Carla said. "Especially the young ones."

"We've been using nights to prepare," Pablo explained. "None of us have slept much this past week."

"But they could track you," Kevin said.

Pablo pointed to a man with a scraggly beard, snoring softly by the nearest tree. "Forrest will know."

"And Hank," Carla added, pointing to the man guarding the horses. "And Tula."

"Forrest is better." Pablo stretched out his legs. "He'll take over next. Even so, my guess is Hollis and his wolves will chase their tails tonight. Come sunrise, we'll be gone."

Kevin asked, "Where to?"

"I was hoping you'd tell us," Pablo replied. "It's why I sent Carla to find you."

"You're their leader."

Pablo shook his head. "I'm just a sergeant. I'm good at what I do. That's not just my rank, it's who I am. I don't have the vision to play officer. Or the smarts."

Carla protested softly, "Pablo. Stop."

"I'm too tired for games." He pointed at the sleeping crew. "They need a safe haven. They need a future where they'll not be treated like the mayor's new weapon. They trust me. I trust you."

Kevin was about to say that he was not the man for the job. That Caleb was the one born to lead, and this conversation solidified their need to head south. But all of that could wait until Pablo and Carla had some much-needed rest. Instead, he asked, "Can you locate someone who's trying to stay hidden?"

Pablo frowned. "Is that someone an adept?"

"Yes. There are three of them, two men and a woman."

"Can they pass on thoughts or feelings?"

"The woman can."

"We've never tried it before, but it might be possible. Where are they?"

"Atlanta, I think."

Carla showed him a worried gaze. "Our group will never walk that far."

"And buying transport for this many will only alert the authorities," Pablo added.

Kevin nodded. He had been thinking the same thing. "I have an idea."

When Kevin woke, the horses were gone.

The three guards last on duty, two young women and a teenage boy, were in tears. None of them could say when the mounts had been taken. All of them insisted they had stayed awake, and Kevin believed them. Or rather, he decided it did not matter. Venting his anger and frustration would not bring the horses back.

The group was slow getting started. They remained fearful around Kevin, as clearly their Charlotte experiences had taught them to be wary of anyone in authority. Kevin could see they were strung out, exhausted, and prone to make mistakes. What was more, the militia was bound to be hunting them. He could think of no way to keep them alive and free except his plan. And the idea seemed very feeble in the light of day.

Even so, Pablo got them up and fed and packed in far less time than Kevin would have imagined possible. When all were ready, they joined the others walking the Refugee Trail.

An hour later, they joined the main route linking Charlotte to points south. The highway had once been two broad asphalt rivers separated by a grassy divide. Now the eastern road was the only one still officially in use. Motorized traffic was light, for fuel remained prohibitively expensive and parts were scarce. More refugees joined them here, fleeing Charlotte and the militia. Kevin spotted a bus heading south from the same terminal where Caleb and Zeke and Hester had departed. There were also a few trucks and official vehicles, but not many, for they soon would be entering the disputed boundary zone.

Charlotte angrily objected to Atlanta joining with Greenville. The region they were now entering had become taut with coming conflict. Even now, on a fresh early summer morning, with not a cloud in the sky or a breath of wind, Kevin could smell the stench of cordite that had not yet been ignited.

After another ten miles or so, most refugees left the main highway, taking a secondary road that aimed them straight south. Kevin explained this to Carla and Pablo as they walked. His training had not included much hard intelligence on what went on south of Atlanta. But some of his fellow deputies, especially those assigned to the southern patrols, talked of little else.

"Five years after the Great Crash," Kevin said, "a sickness spread out from three of the cities south of Atlanta."

"I heard it was the same year as the Crash," Carla said. "And five cities."

Kevin shrugged. From this distance of so many miles and years, it hardly mattered. "They had some name for it, I forget what it was."

"A bacterial infection," Carla supplied. "A strain resistant to antibiotics."

"So maybe you should tell the story."

She shook her head. "I read it in a book. You've seen the aftermath."

Pablo said, "For the rest of us uneducated folk, somebody tell us the rest."

Kevin glanced back to find the group clustered in close, listening. He went on, "The way I heard it, the sickness spread like wildfire."

"The Great Plague, it was called back then," Carla said.

"I've never heard that before."

She shrugged. "Books."

"So what happened?" Pablo demanded.

"The only way it was contained was by sealing off the infected areas." Kevin shook his head, glad he had not been around to endure that duty. "All of Florida south of Jacksonville. The region around what once was a city called Orleans . . ."

"New Orleans," Carla said.

Kevin suspected she knew far more than he did but had not spoken of it because of how troubling it would be to her group, as long as they had nowhere else to go. Now they all looked to Kevin with hope for a new tomorrow. He shuddered at the responsibility cast upon him and went on, "All of Alabama and a lot of the border regions with Mexico. They're still classed as no-man's-lands. Everything else I know is basically rumors."

"Tell me what you've heard," Pablo said.

"The boundary fences aren't patrolled any longer. They haven't been in a generation. We used to meet with deputies from Atlanta and Jacksonville. They call those places dead zones, but only because nobody is coming out."

"So that's where these refugees are headed?" Pablo looked horrified. "A dead zone?"

Kevin nodded. "Maybe it's safe now."

"At least from township militias," Carla said.

They trekked in silence for another mile. As the sun rose, other families emerged from roadside camps. Finally Kevin found what he was looking for, a humpbacked ridge that slowly rose to dominate the left-hand side of the highway. "If we're doing what I suggested, this is where we need to turn off."

Pablo had not spoken since learning the refugees' destination. His voice grated with anger as he said, "Nothing's changed. The weakest of our group can't walk much farther, and we leave no one behind."

Carla set a hand upon her fiancé's shoulder. "Kevin's plan is a good one."

Either her touch or her tone eased him somewhat. Even so, Pablo replied, "I didn't rescue my team to take them to anywhere called a dead zone."

Kevin found himself liking this pair more with every word they spoke. "I couldn't agree more."

He had not been up here since his early days as a trainee. But those events had left an indelible mark. At his signal, they gathered in one of the clearings that had been vacated. No one traveling the road gave them so much as a glance. Gradually they shifted back, farther and farther, until the surrounding pines offered them a shadowed veil. When the road emptied momentarily, Kevin signaled and they moved into the trees.

They trekked through the woods in silence. At least, no one talked. But they made all the noise Kevin expected from twenty untrained people hiking through woodlands. There was no trail, but this was an old-growth forest, mostly hickory and pine and massive oak. Here and there a dogwood extended its white-blossom branches like a beaming welcome to these strangers. The ground was springy-soft with needles and last year's leaves.

The slope was gradual at first. He noticed a subtle change of position, requiring the walkers to lean into the incline, which remained hard to gauge while dodging trees. It became steeper, then slippery as well, until most were puffing hard and groaning. Then ahead of them Kevin spied blue sky through gently waving branches. He turned and signaled them to halt. Most collapsed gratefully to the earth.

Kevin had not taken aim at any specific point. Anywhere along the five-mile ridgeline would do for what he had in mind. He and Pablo left their packs beside Carla and crawled up the final rise.

When they arrived at the top, Pablo surveyed the expanse below them and quietly declared, "It is just as you described."

"You doubted me?"

"Only a little." Behind and below them, the group talked softly and shifted to more comfortable positions. Pablo asked, "Is it okay for them to eat?"

"Yes, but no fire. Tell them to keep their voices soft, and no one can show themselves over the ledge."

Pablo passed word, then returned with a handful of nuts and berries. When Kevin shook his head at the offer, he asked, "You're not hungry?"

He was, but the climb had caused his leg to throb worse than ever. "Not just yet."

Behind them, the group clustered and passed canteens and sacks of food. Kevin saw no need to order them to strict silence. Their target was a road at the base of the hill, over a hundred meters from where he crouched. He kept his own head below the tall weeds, rising for an occasional glimpse in both directions. The target area was completely empty.

Pablo returned to crouch beside him. "What now?"

Kevin settled back and rubbed his leg above the wound. The pain reached all the way to his knee now. He could only hope the doctor had been correct and there was no risk of infection. He glanced over the edge. The ground below them remained silent, empty.

He replied, "Now we wait."

...

After a time, Carla climbed the rise to join them. With her was Forrest, the best of their so-called trackers. She offered them a canteen of sweet tea, which helped settle Kevin's turbulent gut. He refused part of a steak sandwich but managed some of the dried fruit.

Carla asked, "How long must we wait?"

"Hard to say. I haven't been here in quite a while." Kevin pointed north. "A few miles up is the main militia barracks and training center at Fort Mills. Any detail patrolling the Greenville region has to pass us here."

She accepted the news by turning and looking back over

the tree line to the unseen highway. "So many displaced," she murmured.

Kevin asked, "Do you know why the hunt for adepts went into high gear?"

"Rumors only." Pablo kept his gaze on the empty road below. "The Washington bureaucrats sent to control the roadblock and internment camp . . ."

He went quiet because a woman in her thirties crept up the hill until she was close enough to offer Kevin a flirtatious grin. "My, but you're a big boy. Pablo, aren't you going to introduce us?"

"Kevin, this is Doris. Doris, we're talking."

She sniffed at his attempt to dismiss her and said to Kevin, "I saw you limping, hon. What happened?"

Kevin disliked admitting to any weakness, especially now. But his injury was real, and they needed to know. "Bear trap."

"Oh, excellent. Not that you were hurt. But I might be able to help."

Pablo protested, "We can't have Kevin collapsing on us."

"Pablo, stop," Carla said.

Doris asked, "How long ago did you get hurt?"

"Five days," Kevin said.

"Better and better. Show me."

By the time Kevin had rolled up his trouser leg and unwrapped the bandage, a number of the others had shifted position so they could watch.

Doris had surprisingly strong hands. She prodded, then shut her eyes, clenched her face up tight, and probed deeper.

"Ouch."

"Shush now." She opened her eyes and looked at Carla. "You'll have someone carry me?"

"Of course."

"And my pack. I don't want to lose the pictures of my nieces." To Kevin she said, "I'm told this hurts rather a lot."

Kevin arched his back and took a two-fisted grip on the earth as his wound began to burn.

...

Twenty minutes later, they were still waiting. Not that Kevin minded the delay. His leg throbbed fiercely. Yet there was a clear difference to what he had felt before Doris's treatment, and this made the pain bearable.

He remained sprawled on the hill's crest where Doris had worked on his wound. He glanced down the ridge, back to where she lay in the shade of a massive oak, snoring gently.

Pablo had resumed his place beside Kevin and asked, "Can you walk?"

"I think so. We'll know soon enough."

"Some of those Doris works on moan for days."

"I believe it." Kevin drank from his canteen. And resumed watching the empty road.

When the conflict with Atlanta had started to heat up, the militia's main headquarters and officers' residences were moved to the city's southern boundary, a village once known as Pineville. They were soon joined by a number of businesses and merchants who relied on the militia for their trade. A market grew along the former main street, elegant enough to draw Charlotte's wealthy. Pineville and the main barracks in Fort Mills were connected to the southern highway by the road that Kevin scouted.

The watcher sprawled on Pablo's other side hissed quietly. Forrest was a portly man in his late thirties, prematurely bald, and clearly unaccustomed to any kind of exercise. He said, "Vehicles coming our way."

Pablo asked, "How many?"

"Three trucks. And a car." A pause, then, "And a lot of guns."

Pablo said, "A military convoy."

Kevin asked, "You can tell if they're armed?"

Forrest nodded. His head was cocked to one side as though he listened to unseen winds. "They're coming fast."

Ten silent minutes passed. Finally Kevin heard a faint rumbling to the north. He risked another glance, then said, "I see them."

There were four vehicles in the convoy, a boxy lead car followed by three large trucks. Because of the good weather, the canvas tops were pulled back to show rear holds filled with uniformed militia. The central hold of each truck was piled with gear and supplies and weapons.

"Sixty militia plus officers," Pablo muttered. "Where are they headed?"

Kevin was stumped. Most of the disputed territory south of them was now firmly under the control of Atlanta. Their militia force had to number twice those of Charlotte, perhaps even three times. There was no logic to such a convoy. Patrolling with this large a force was an invitation to war.

He forced his attention back to the matter at hand. He looked at the two newcomers stationed beside Forrest. Barry was a fresh-faced man in his late teens whose pale features were covered by freckles. Beside him knelt Tula, a slender, dark-skinned woman in her midtwenties, lovely in the manner of a bruised rose.

Kevin asked, "Can you take out just the middle truck?"

In reply, Barry shut his eyes. His features tightened in concentration.

A moment later, shouts rose from down below as the center truck ground to a halt.

The rear truck started blowing its horn. The lead truck stopped and gave its horn a long hoot. Finally the car halted and reversed back. All the doors opened.

"That's Hollis," Kevin said.

...

If their survival had not hung in the balance, Kevin would have found Hollis's response comic. The militia captain stomped about the road, shouting at the three men who were now huddled under the truck's raised hood. Troops sprawled along the road's verge or leaned against the trucks, smoking and talking softly. A card game started. Hollis continued to strut and shout.

"Perfect," Kevin said. Barry and Tula grinned in response.

His first alert at wrongness was when Pablo hissed, "It's them."

His words and his tense expression were enough to send Forrest and Tula scooting down the ridge. Barry flattened to the earth as Pablo slipped back and called softly to his group, "Three Watchers. Everybody quiet. For your lives."

The trio emerging from the lead vehicle wore black suits, black shirts buttoned to their necks, black sunglasses. They carried identical cases by straps hanging from their left shoulders. Kevin lowered his head down to where the high grass served as a veil. Behind him was the stillness of terror. The only sound came from a cardinal high in a neighboring treetop. Kevin kept observing because he was not a special or adept or whatever they wanted to call themselves. And he needed to understand.

Hollis walked over to where the trio stood. The captain's words did not carry, but the message was clear enough. He jammed his finger down the southern road, then pointed at the sky. Whatever these bureaucrats intended, they and the truck were putting Hollis off schedule.

The dark-suited trio might as well have been deaf, for all the notice they gave the militia captain. One of them turned to the others and spoke. Only then did Kevin realize it was a woman. She was almost as tall as the two men and dressed identically. But as she turned her head Kevin saw the cut of her hair, the soft jawline, her full lips. All Hollis saw was her utter lack of interest in him or his schedule. He barked something and stomped away.

The trio opened their leather pouches and pulled out identical headsets. The apparatuses were made of some shiny material and fit tightly over their hair. The three settled grey spectacles down over their eyes. A stubby tube protruded from the center of their foreheads. At a word from the woman, they touched a spot above their right temple, then began sweeping the surrounding forests and hills.

Kevin crept down beside Pablo. And held his breath.

According to the driver who took Caleb south, Atlanta's Ritz Hotel was a genuine palace with prices to match.

The driver talked constantly through the first hour of their journey south. Caleb had never met anyone like this man. He lied with every breath. Caleb's truth sense had kicked in almost the same moment he had shut his door, even before the driver started the engine. Which was interesting, given how the price had been set in advance and then written down at Hester's insistence. Half was paid before they set out. Even so, the portly man behind the wheel continued to breathe in, lie, breathe in, lie. Even his jolly mood was false.

Finally Caleb leaned forward so as to speak to Hester in the front passenger seat. "Stay on guard."

Hester's face tightened into a series of hard edges. "You got something?"

"I think . . . Yes."

That was enough for Hester. She turned to the driver and ordered, "Stop the car."

"That's difficult here, little lady." The man shot her a big grin. "Up ahead we've got the sweetest little spot, you'll think you've died and gone—"

"Zeke."

The knife flashed gold in the afternoon light. Zeke slipped forward and pressed it to the driver's neck. "Do what the lady says."

"Th-the car is registered and the militia are my very best friends—"

"We're not stealing anything," Caleb said. When the car pulled into the weeds and stopped, he said, "Open the trunk."

Hester was already moving. "Stay on him, Zeke."

Caleb walked around back and waited as she opened the hard case they had purchased to hold their guns. She handed him both a rifle and a pistol and took the same for herself. They checked the loads, then Caleb carried a second pair back for Zeke.

The driver sweated profusely at the sight of the guns. "That's highly illegal."

"So is highway robbery," Hester said. She cocked her rifle noisily, then settled the barrel on the armrest between her and the driver. "Tell me I have your full attention."

"Absolutely, ma'am."

She reached into her pocket and flashed her badge. The sight of the guard's shield caused the driver to wince. "If you stop for any reason between now and the hotel, you die. If you slow for a roadblock, you die. If you have a flat tire, tell me what happens."

"I-I die."

"Zeke, Caleb, roll down your windows and show the world your weapons." She leaned back. "Let's go."

Twice during the remainder of their journey, the driver sounded his horn and flashed his lights. When Hester demanded to know what he was doing, his only response was, "Keeping you folks safe."

Kevin's team remained frozen in place for well over an hour. Down below, the Charlotte militia relaxed along either side of the road. Work on the middle truck had ceased. Finally the three dark-suited visitors pulled off their helmets and clustered by the front vehicle. Hollis glared at them repeatedly but remained silent.

At a gesture from Kevin, Pablo crawled back up the ridge. He sighed with relief when he saw the trio had stopped their hunt. He softly called to the others, "We're safe."

Kevin thought the claim was premature but did not object, because the entire group relaxed. A few smiles even surfaced. He asked softly, "How do they track specials?"

"Adepts," Pablo corrected without heat. He used his chin to point at the trio. "From what I've heard, those apparatuses allow them to detect two elements that are said to be different about us. First, our temperature is elevated by more than a degree. This heat signature is detected by the devices that cover their eyes. We are said to shine far more brilliantly than . . ."

"Normal people," Kevin suggested.

Pablo shrugged. "What is normal in this day and age?"

"And the second element?"

"The central component detects brain-wave activity. Ours is different. Or so I am told. But again, this is all from rumors whispered at midnight by some very frightened people."

"How did they find you and Carla?"

"They restrained me, not her. We were entering Charlotte's main food market. The militia had the checkpoint, same as usual, searching everybody. One moment Carla and I stood waiting to be inspected, me carrying her basket, the next I was plucked from the line and stuffed inside a truck, my ankle chained to the running board."

Kevin tried to make sense of it. "Charlotte probably worked out some way to check body temperature without Washington's help."

"There was a metal detector," Pablo recalled. "There always is."

Kevin mulled that over as he watched Hollis bark orders down below. A group of six soldiers, two from each truck, pulled rations from the back of the vehicles and passed them around. He realized he was hungry and that his leg did not hurt as much as before. "So Carla wasn't taken."

"No. She remained free."

Kevin decided that issue could wait. "What happened after that?"

"We were housed in a compound." Pablo's features resumed their pinched look. "One by one we were taken out. Eight never came back. Then you and Carla arrived."

Kevin's next question was halted by Forrest, who crawled partway up the slope and whispered, "More trucks. Three of them."

That was what Kevin had been hoping for. "Ready the team," he said. "And pass me something to eat."

Twenty minutes later, three more trucks trundled down the highway. These were far larger than the troop carriers, and each held mountains of equipment—poles long as tree trunks, bales of wire, tools, and barrels of what Kevin assumed were nails. An entire vehicle was filled with sheets of sawn board. Following them was another troop carrier.

They watched as Hollis redistributed the troops from the stricken vehicle. Kevin noticed Pablo's expression had become very grave. "What's wrong?"

"I don't know where they're headed," Pablo replied. "But I'm certain of their purpose."

Kevin watched as Hollis stomped to the front vehicle, called to the others, waved his arm, and slipped into the front passenger seat. The convoy drove slowly away, leaving the lone truck behind.

"They're building an internment camp," Pablo said. "To corral the adepts those Washington suits identify. The same duty I ran from."

Kevin remained where he was as the convoy rumbled into the distance. Something this large had been planned out well in advance. But he had to figure the timing had been accelerated. The only other explanation for how this move followed so closely on Pablo's escape was coincidence. Sheriff Ferguson had always said coincidence was just a threat in disguise.

His thoughts were interrupted by Forrest sidling up and handing over a canteen and sack of dried fruit. Kevin ate a handful and asked, "Anything coming our way?"

Forrest lifted his head as if sniffing the wind. "All clear."

Kevin remained where he was, thinking while he ate.

Pablo said, "Leg better?"

"Much." He took one more handful, then passed back the sack. "We have to assume they'll form a blockade this side of Greenville. Maybe two. One on the main highway, the other on the Refugee Trail."

"What do we do?"

Kevin flattened the ground between them and began to draw. "We're here, south by west of Charlotte. Greenville is farther in the same direction. From there, it's a straight line southwest to Atlanta. All this stretch between here and the Atlanta boundary is heavily patrolled."

Pablo said, "We need to pick up supplies. We have enough for one more good meal. Two if we ration."

Carla was near enough to hear. She added, "The little ones need something warm to eat."

"We all do," Pablo said. "It's been a hard few days."

And bound to get harder still, Kevin suspected, but saw no need to say it aloud. "Can your team stifle communications like they do engines and lights?"

"Our team," Forrest said. "I like the sound of that."

"Absolutely," Pablo said. "But they need a specific target."

Kevin rose slowly, testing his leg. He glanced down at the team, all of whom were watching him now. All but Doris, who remained conked out beneath the oak tree. "Time to move."

....

The road took hold and swept them south.

That was how it seemed to Kevin. Within the first hour of them loading into the militia truck, the road felt like the destination they had been aiming for all along. They avoided the main Greenville–Atlanta highway and instead aimed almost straight south. The route Kevin took was little more than a rutted track, a shadowy reminder of what once had been a grand thoroughfare. Trees and stubborn weeds were eating into the dual ribbons from both sides. They passed two farm wagons, whose passengers eyed them with open-mouthed astonishment. As though their presence was so absurd, the truck and its passengers had to be a mirage. Otherwise the highway and the day was theirs.

Following the Great Crash and the sickness that followed, any number of cities had simply vanished. Their names became faint reminders of all that had been lost. Kevin had spent hours poring over old maps, trying to piece together an image of the world that had once been America. Forgotten places called to him, like Spartanburg and Lexington and Augusta. Sheriff Ferguson shared his passion, but for different reasons. Gus saw himself as bound together with other like-minded lawmen who refused to give in to the bad ways. *Rule of law* was a favorite saying of his. All laws must be applied equally to all members of the population. Wealth and political position change nothing as far as the law is concerned. Gus repeated the words like a chant, embedding them deep in Kevin's young mind. *Rule of law.*

The regions east of Atlanta were lawless terrain now. Some farming communities still held stubbornly to land that had been in their families for centuries. They paid levies to clans who fought and marauded at will. Which was why the central government in Washington made no complaint about Atlanta's land grab. At least the city's expansion brought the region into a semblance of order. Gus had spoken of such actions with the contempt and hatred of a man who took such lawlessness as a personal affront.

Kevin's plan was to circle east of the Refugee Trail, then rejoin it south of the Atlanta boundary. The problem was, their truck was new, and thus a tempting target for bandits who controlled the highway. Which was why Pablo remained standing in the truck's rear hold, rather than seated up front with Carla and Forrest.

The empty reaches through which they drove worked upon them all. The truck remained eerily silent as they ground their way south. Kevin could not risk driving faster than a horse might trot, for the pavement was riven in places with gashes so deep the bottom was lost to shadows. Even so, he pressed on as fast as he could. The sun's passage clocked him. They could not risk being caught on this highway after dark.

Two hours and a bit after they took the road, Forrest said, "People ahead. And guns."

He said it in such a conversational tone, Kevin needed a moment to realize what it meant. He shouted through the open rear window, "Pablo!"

"Here."

"Forrest just raised the alarm."

Pablo crouched down and inserted his head into the rear cab window. "Tell me."

"A lot of them," Forrest said. His eyes were shut now, his features tight with concentration. "Twenty or more. They've built a barricade across the road."

The bandits had chosen their position well. The highway traversed a narrow valley, with forest sweeping down to gnaw at the asphalt from either side. Up ahead the road curved gently, the route lost to trees and shadows.

But Pablo didn't seem the least bit worried. "Now you're going to see an astonishment."

Kevin asked, "Should I slow?"

"What for?" He straightened and pounded on the cab's roof. "Hold to your course and speed!"

Kevin was about to protest when the barricade came into view. It was fashioned from rusting vehicles and fallen trees, with a single narrow passage blocked by a gate on old tires. Guns sprouted along the entire length of the fortification.

A man and a woman, both dressed in brown homespun and boots and wide-brimmed hats, stepped around the gate. The man held a hunting rifle, the woman a small-gauge shotgun. The man raised his hand, ordering them to stop. The woman lifted her weapon and aimed it straight at Kevin.

Pablo called, "Dale?"

A voice far too young to be their only line of defense shouted, "Ready!"

"Now!"

To Kevin's eye, the entire mass of people and guns and fencing became caught up by an invisible plow.

There were shouts and roars of anger and shrill screams as the people were swept aside with their barricade. Some of the bandits managed to get off shots, but they all went wide, save for the lead woman's buckshot. Kevin winced as a pellet punched through the windshield just above his left ear. The bursts rattled against the hood and took out their right headlight.

Then the battle of the Augusta highway was over, as quickly as it had begun.

Vehicles and people and weapons were rammed into the tree line on either side of the road. The trees themselves shivered in protest as they absorbed the entire mess.

"Keep pushing!" Pablo shouted.

As Kevin drove past, he saw how the closest trees were bending and cracking as they gradually leaned farther back. He accelerated as fast as he dared. The cries and shouts grew steadily fainter, then vanished into the distance.

Kevin drove them through good farmland, well-watered and rich. He watched the farmers stop their late-afternoon chores and peer worriedly at the passing truck. They crossed the Saluda River south of Lake Greenwood, then turned west, taking a road that had been reduced to little more than a rutted memory. As the sun touched the western treetops, they entered the Atlanta version of Overpass, an immigrant haven called Farmers Market.

They did not stop, however. Not yet. Instead they followed a well-used trail that headed toward the Savannah River. They halted near dusk by a well-tended house and garden, with songbirds greeting the rising moon and a lamp in every window. When the farmer and his wife emerged onto their front porch, Kevin saw how neither carried a weapon. He took that as a sign they were now close enough to Atlanta for folk to feel safe.

For payment in advance, the team was permitted to camp by the barn, use the well and bathhouse, and cook on the outdoor stove. Kevin then paid more silver to borrow three of the farmer's horses and a mule. The farmer did not ask why Kevin preferred not to take the truck into the market town. Instead, he walked around the truck once, took in the Charlotte militia shield that had been scratched out, touched the points where shotgun pellets had taken bites from the hood and windshield and one headlight, then walked back to the house without another word.

Kevin was as tired as he had ever been. Tired in the manner that left him feeling old. But he had known any number of such hours, when a day's duty as Overpass deputy had been followed by a night of transporting refugees, then another day on patrol. He did not fight the fatigue. He simply shouldered it as yet another burden.

Pablo wanted to come with him into town, of course, but Kevin insisted he remain with the team. He selected a young woman named Irene, whose ability was communicating with certain others over long distances. Irene was in her early twenties, with an abundance of unruly blonde hair and lips the color of a ripe peach. She carried herself like a dancer, long limbed and incredibly erect. She was quiet in the manner of one who did not need either a voice or words to communicate. Kevin thought her the loveliest of the crew, and the most feminine.

Pablo wanted him to also take Dale, the young man who had saved them on the road. But Kevin was adamant. The last thing they needed was to reveal their presence. When Pablo demanded to know what Kevin would do if trouble erupted, he did not respond. In truth he intended to send word through Irene and sacrifice himself for the team. But there was no benefit to be gained from arguing. So he simply saddled two of the rented horses and set off.

When Kevin and Irene reached the market's main road, they joined a parade of families. Kevin had often seen this when working with refugees, how the hour was less important than the need. Many actually preferred the night for such activities. Daylight in public places risked exposure.

As they approached Farmers Market, the moon shone upon a boisterous village. Guards patrolling the periphery directed Kevin to a corral, where he rented space in a stable. When he asked about stowing their purchased items with the horses, the trader pointed to his own armed guards, then showed Kevin other stalls where slumbering children and piles of goods lined the interior walls.

The night was utterly clear, and the town held a carnival air. Patrons crammed the tables of taverns rimming the market, while jugglers and musicians plied their trade for tossed pennies. The air was redolent with the fragrance of roasting meat. Kevin bought two flatbreads crammed with lamb and chopped greens and asked directions to the stalls selling fresh produce.

He and Irene ate as they walked. The prices were outrageous, and none of the merchants appeared willing to bargain. When their canvas sacks grew heavy, they retraced their steps to the stall. Twice more they returned and stowed their goods. Entire families had joined the children in surrounding stalls, slumbering with their mounts. The barn's guards were vigilant and wary. Kevin decided to make one more trip, then bed down in the straw for the night.

As they returned to the market a third time, Irene surprised him by asking, "Does it bother you, my silence?"

Kevin liked having a reason to stare at her. She was easy on the eyes. "Not at all."

"Most men I've known, they find it unsettling."

"You've known a lot of men, have you?"

She smiled with her entire face. "I've known enough."

"You should smile more often," Kevin said, and turned back to the road.

Five minutes later, as they reentered the food lanes, the night erupted.

The screams and shouts were so faint at first, they could easily have passed as merely a discordant note in the night's clamor. But Kevin had heard such alarm before. He knew at gut level that the market was under attack.

He and Irene had been buying a load of cabbages, inspecting each for worms or rot. He ordered her to stay where she was and headed swiftly down the road, hunting the source. That was what he had been trained for, and the biggest difference between his kind and most others. Lawmen ran toward trouble instead of away from it.

The closer he came, the stronger the human tide surged against him. He expected to find either Atlanta's militia or the market's guards hunting a thief. Then he rounded a corner, and up ahead he saw the green and black uniforms of Charlotte's troops.

The sight was enough to shift Kevin into high gear. He slipped into a tight alcove between two stalls. His thoughts kept pace with his frantic search for a weapon. Hollis and the Charlotte mayor would use the Washington hunters as their excuse. They were here under orders from Washington.

It was a feeble claim. But Hollis and his men being this far south, in such numbers, meant their goal was more important than all the underlying risks.

They were hunting Kevin's team.

The stalls to either side of Kevin had cloth walls held in place by ropes tied to steel rods pounded into the earth. He used his belt knife to cut the line, then hauled first one and then a second rod from the earth. They were slightly longer than his forearm and weighed about five pounds each.

He did not hide so much as allow the shadows to swallow him. The crowd grew denser and more frantic, being shifted against their will, protesting and fearful. Then the enemy came into view.

The first line of Charlotte militia was composed of three men. Kevin was mildly surprised to see Hollis had paraded them in full dress uniform. He had to assume Hollis and Silas Fleming were using this excuse to do what they had wanted all along. Pick a fight with Atlanta that its mayor could not ignore.

The three guards were equipped with electric lanterns strapped tightly to their chests, leaving their hands and arms free. The lights illuminated a wide swath of the avenue and shops to either side. They carried two clubs each and waved them back and forth, like shepherds shifting reluctant beasts.

Kevin watched as one of the stallholders, a barrel-shaped man with a jutting black beard, stepped forward and waved his arms in protest. He shouted something about Atlanta and tribute and legality. The trooper on the left side reached out and touched him with one of the clubs. Just a touch, little more than a soft jab. There was a hiss, and the man screamed shrilly and jerked. Kevin had heard of these prods and their electric jolts. The man stumbled and would have gone down, had not another man plucked him up and pulled him along, joining the frantic, jostling crowd.

Behind the trio walked another trooper, this one armed with a rifle. A more tightly focused light was attached to the barrel's scope-mount. The soldier swept his weapon back and forth in practiced arcs.

Kevin found himself resuming the same tight focus that had seen him through so many dangerous moments. Gradually the clamor faded away until he no longer heard the shouts and protests and wailing children and bleating animals. He took note of the tendrils of smoke that drifted overhead and knew at some vague level that a cooking stall had caught fire. But all his attention was now fastened upon the four approaching troopers. Rage built inside him, and for once he welcomed it.

Kevin timed his approach so he was moving the instant the rifle strobe swept by. He followed the light, hoping the frontline troops' vision would be momentarily impaired. He felt as though he glided over the earth rather than taking the four steps required to bring him up to the left-hand guard. His adrenaline-stoked brain was able to parse each breath, such that he had time to wonder if this was how a great hunting cat felt, being granted momentary wings as it flew in for the kill.

His sudden appearance caused the trooper to jerk back. He was a bullish man in his late thirties, five inches shorter and probably fifty pounds heavier than Kevin, and was slow to respond. Having a civilian suddenly appear in combat mode was clearly the absolute last thing he expected. Kevin brought his left arm across his body. The steel rod struck the man's head with a solid and satisfying *thunk*.

Long before the man ended his spasm and started his fall, Kevin had shifted to the middle guard. He moved his right hand, swinging in a spiral, almost a dance. He continued shifting to his right while impacting the trooper's temple. He had no time to check his work or make sure the guard was down. He had to trust the impact that had resonated up to his shoulder. Everything depended on speed.

Luckily the right-hand guard was a green recruit, freckle faced and so young Kevin doubted he shaved regularly. And scared. The guard's eyes were two saucers at the realization of what was coming his way. Kevin hammered the guy square in the middle of his forehead. His eyelids fluttered and his arms tried to bring up his weapons, but his brain had already shut down.

Then the spotlight found Kevin.

He moved by reflex born from a hundred hard hours on the Overpass live-fire training course. He dropped and rolled.

The space where he had been was illuminated first by the strobe and then by the cracking rifle.

The crowd's panic reached an entirely new level. What before had been a disorderly rush became a stampede.

Kevin dropped the rod in his left hand, gripped the earth, and leapt forward. The soldier probably expected him to rise, for his aim remained slightly high. But Kevin had no intention of straightening. Instead, he slammed the rod with all his force into the trooper's left shin.

There was a sharp crack, then the trooper screamed and dropped to the earth. Before he could aim his weapon, Kevin brought the rod down on his head.

Kevin wanted to stop and take a single frantic breath. He wanted to fit his heart back inside his chest. He wanted to give his trembling limbs a chance to recover. But the shouts rising from lanes to either side told him there was no time.

He ripped the rifle from the trooper's limp grip, unholstered the sidearm, then scrambled back to the three prone and groaning militia. He gathered up their clubs and lights and revolvers. Then he rose in swift stages. In front of him, the crowd sensed a change. First a few and then a dozen and then more and more realized the lane behind them had become free of the enemy.

They surged back down the lane, away from whatever it was the militia had been pointing them toward.

Kevin shoved his way through the throng, his arms filled with weapons and lights. To his vast relief, Irene remained where he had left her. He motioned her forward and shouted, "Run!"

An hour after sunset, Caleb's vehicle halted at Atlanta's boundary roadblock. The militia officer surveyed Hester's badge, then handed out passes and ordered them to stow their weapons in the trunk.

The main road leading downtown was illuminated by electric lights. Caleb stared at the wrought-iron towers and the brilliant yellow globes, fearing the risk he took entering here. The hotel grounds were rimmed by a tall concrete wall topped by barbed wire and more electric lights. The entrance was guarded, and the guards appropriated all their weapons.

The Ritz Hotel's lobby was unlike anything Caleb had ever imagined. One grand chamber led into another, all lit by crystal chandeliers. He, Zeke, and Hester each carried two bags, one for clothes and another for the gold. Empty rifle cases were slung from their shoulders.

As he approached the reception desk, Caleb caught sight of himself in a pair of floor-to-ceiling mirrors. He found himself arrested by the sight of a stranger staring back at him. His dark blond hair was precisely cut. His crisp new shirt was grey flecked with slate and heightened the breadth of his shoulders. Black trousers fell on polished black boots. Caleb searched the weary gaze staring back at him and wished he could feel that he belonged as much as he appeared.

The desk clerk had been alerted by the night porter and the security guard that a private car was depositing guests. Despite the hour, he offered Caleb his very best smile. "How might I help you, sir?"

Caleb knew what to ask for because Hester had coached him. "Do you have a suite?"

"Most certainly, sir." He surveyed the pair who now waited behind him. "But we also have servants' housing in the cellar."

"My bodyguard stays with me," Caleb replied. "And my servant can sleep on the floor."

...

When they were in the suite with the door locked, Caleb's first words were, "We've got one chance to get this right. All I can see are the problems. What if I've forgotten something?"

Zeke shrugged. "You probably have."

"Oh, that makes me feel so much better."

"That's why you have us," Hester said. "To guard your back."

"And we're good at it," Zeke said.

She glanced at him. "One of us is, anyway."

He grinned. "Hey, thanks."

Hester said to Caleb, "I'm tired and I'm filthy. I have first dibs on the bath, and you youngsters can work out the sleeping arrangements. We can all worry tomorrow."

...

The next morning they feasted on Caleb's first buffet breakfast. He had been raised on potluck dinners, but this was entirely different. The hotel's vast dining hall had more white-uniformed waiters than guests. There was enough food on display to feed the Catawba enclave. He felt scandalized by the waste.

When they could eat no more, Caleb remained where he was, trapped by doubts.

Finally Hester leaned across the table and said, "It's a good plan."

Zeke said, "She's right."

Hester's gaze remained steady on Caleb. "It's time to move. You ready?"

"Maddie is waiting," Caleb told himself.

"There you go." She rose to her feet. "One step in front of the other. That's how good plans become great."

Caleb went to the front desk and asked to see the manager. When the older gentleman appeared, Caleb said, "I need to ask you about a private matter."

The man was dressed in pin-striped trousers, dark silk tie, and a black vest with gold buttons. The oil in his greying hair reflected the chandelier's illumination as he bowed. "Certainly, sir. Right this way."

Caleb motioned for Hester to remain where she was and followed the man behind the counter. When the door to his office was shut, Caleb came right to the point. "I need a list of honest lawyers."

The manager took his time seating himself. "Define honest."

Caleb was ready for that. "Somebody I can rely on when I'm seven hundred miles away."

"Then it will be a very short list indeed." The manager thought for a moment, or pretended to. "Of course, such information carries a significant value."

"Absolutely," Caleb agreed. "I was thinking a silver bar's worth."

The manager proved able to remain genteel even when dickering. "Two would perhaps be more fitting, sir."

"Done," Caleb replied. "But only if they'll see me today."

■■■

When Caleb and the others returned upstairs, Caleb carried a sheet of paper with five names. Hester and Zeke remained silent until the suite's door was locked. Then Hester demanded, "How do you pick the right one?"

"It's already done," Caleb replied.

Zeke crowded in close. "You already sense the one we need to contact?"

"Soon as the manager wrote down the name," Caleb replied. He indicated the cases holding the gold. "All of that comes with us."

Two objectives had been at the heart of Caleb's planning since leaving Catawba. Finding Maddie and finding a haven for the gold. As intertwined as a living rope.

Distance was not enough to shield Catawba. They needed to find a way to remain protected once news of the gold surfaced. Which it was bound to, sooner or later. Word of this much new wealth was going to emerge. When it did, Catawba's mine had to remain both shielded and secret. Especially after they left to return home. And more important still, when they returned with the next load.

This entire journey came down to controlling risk and using his gifts. The time for hiding was over. He needed to stop taking baby steps. He needed to start testing his boundaries.

Caleb left Zeke and Hester in the hallway by the door

bearing the lawyer's name. He set his own case down beside theirs and entered empty-handed.

The law offices of Hamlin Turner held a shabby, somewhat careless air. As though the attorney was too busy wielding authority to bother with such trifles as a good airing. The outer office was as large as Caleb's entire home. A waiting area extended to the right of the entrance. Waist-high shelves filled with ledgers and files created mock office areas for the three assistants, two men and a woman. The ornate desks were piled high with papers and forms and yellow folders. The oil paintings on the walls were dusty, and several were slightly skewed. The expensive carpet was frayed at the edges, and the broad-planked floor was in need of varnish. Eight people clustered in tight conversation on the sofas and chairs looked up and frowned when Caleb stepped inside.

Caleb selected the woman because she was seated closest to the double doors leading to the inner sanctum. She spared him a single three-second glance as he crossed the broad carpet. By the time he arrived at her desk she had dismissed him and returned to her work.

"Yes?" she asked.

"I need to see Mr. Turner."

"Do you have an appointment?"

"The manager of the Ritz Carlton placed the call."

"Ah. That was you, was it." The woman sniffed softly. "I'll tell you the same thing I said when he called. Mr. Turner could not possibly meet with you until tomorrow at the very earliest, and only then if there is a legal matter of such vital—"

"I need to see him now."

Up close her grey bun had the severe tension of a clenched fist. "That, I'm afraid, is out of the question."

Caleb kept his voice calm, steady, and very soft. "Just the same, ma'am. Mr. Turner will want to see me."

"Is that so." She inspected him more carefully. "What is your name, young man?"

"I can't tell you."

"You can't . . ." She squinted at him. Caleb assumed she was trying to decide whether he was mocking her. "And why not?"

"Because," he replied. "I'm not going to start our business together with a lie."

Her eyes flashed with a glimmer—he hoped it was humor. "Well then. What could you possibly reveal that will result in Mr. Turner giving you the time of day?"

By now the entire office was watching them. But it could not be helped. "Could you please step outside?"

She folded her hands on her papers. "You are asking me to leave the office."

"For thirty seconds. Less. Please."

She inspected him for a time, then rose from her seat. "Lead the way."

One of her associates asked, "Should I call security?"

"Are you a threat, young man?" she asked Caleb.

"Absolutely not."

"I will be right back." She stepped through the outer door, shut it firmly, then demanded, "Now what is this all about?"

"Zeke."

Zeke was already opening his case. He pulled out a burlap packet and handed it to Caleb.

Caleb offered it to the woman. "Give this to Mr. Turner."

Hester added, "Hide it under your coat when you go back inside."

Zeke said, "No one else can know. Including the other office staff."

"Thousands of lives depend upon maintaining secrecy," Hester said.

But the woman made no move to accept the packet. "What on earth do you have there?"

Caleb took Zeke's knife, cut the twine, and opened the burlap. He watched the woman's eyes go round at the sight. "Tell Mr. Turner this is our calling card."

The stables were locked when Kevin and Irene made it back. The owner and his wife watched with weapons propped on the balcony railing as the guards let them enter. Most of the other stalls were already emptied of people and horses and goods. Fast as they could, he and Irene lashed all their sacks onto the horses. Kevin stowed the militia's items in a burlap sack he tied to his saddle horn. But the night and the market chaos were their friends. They joined the refugees and traders pushing out in every direction. Twice in the distance Kevin heard gunfire. But they were not challenged.

The farther they rode from Farmers Market, the quieter the night became. By the time they turned off onto the country trail leading back to where their team bivouacked, they had the route to themselves.

Irene maintained her normal silence, speaking only twice.

The first time, she said no one seemed to be focused upon hunting them, or even searching in this general direction. Kevin started to ask how she knew, but then he left the question unspoken. Now that the danger was past, his body felt flooded with banked-up fatigue. His leg throbbed in the manner of a healing wound. His head thumped in time to his limb. His eyelids weighed a ton each.

The second time Irene spoke was to warn him they had just passed the farm's turnoff. When they entered the main yard, Kevin slipped from the horse's back, stumbled into the barn, found an empty horse stall, and was asleep before his head touched the straw.

It was early afternoon the next day before Kevin awoke. Someone had draped a horse blanket over him while he'd slept. He knew it was late because of how the sun shone through slats on the barn's western side. Rich smells of wood smoke and cooking drifted through the barn's open doors. He heard birdsong, then a young man's laughter. When he stepped into the yard, Pablo greeted him with a bar of soap and a length of sacking. He directed Kevin to shower stalls used by farm workers during the harvest. Kevin reveled in the sensation of being clean, despite the water's shocking cold. He remained there until the shivers forced him to retreat, then dressed in clean clothes from his pack.

When he emerged, Irene walked over bearing a mug. "Feel better?"

"Extremely." He accepted the mug, took a grateful sip. The tea was just as he liked it, strong enough to melt the spoon, a lot of milk, a trace of sugar. "Perfect."

"I know." She smiled at him as Tula walked over with a thick farmer's sandwich. "The wife came out this morning with two fresh loaves, butter, tin plates for us to eat from, and a wedge of cheese she'd made herself. And news the Atlanta garrison has been called north."

Kevin felt a faint stirring of unease, one he could not identify. He surveyed the farmyard and his team as he ate but found no reason for his disquiet. The bread was excellent, the cheese even better.

"She also lent us a big pot," Irene said. "We're making stew with what you brought. It's almost ready."

He thanked her and realized all the others were watching them. Pablo waved to him from his guard position out by the rear well. Kevin lifted his mug in reply.

Tula asked, "More tea?"

"That would be great."

"He likes it with too much milk and not enough sugar," Irene said. When Tula moved off, Irene added, "They're very grateful for what you did."

"I imagine bringing you back safely means as much as having fresh food," Kevin said.

"Taking our side in a fight means the most of all," she replied. "They need a leader."

There it was again. The label that left him staring at the gaping void ahead of them all. How could he be called that when he had no idea where they were going? He turned from that by asking, "Did you sleep okay?"

"Time and again I flashed awake over how close we came to not getting out." She tilted her head, as though needing to inspect him from a different angle. "You weren't scared last night, were you?"

"Absolutely. I was petrified."

"No you weren't."

"Can you read minds?"

"Not like you mean. I can't tell what people are thinking. But I get . . . impressions."

"Like how a guy likes his tea."

Irene offered him a full-lipped smile. "Now you're making fun of me."

"Only a little."

Tula returned with a fresh mug and said, "John wants to have a word."

"John?"

As if in reply, the farmer appeared around the barn's corner and walked over with outstretched hand. "John Handy."

"Kevin Ritter."

"Want to thank you for bringing my horses back unharmed."

Kevin waved for Pablo to join them. "They're good animals."

"That they are. Heard you had yourselves a ruckus in town."

"Do you have any idea why the Charlotte militia would make a sweep?"

"Stirring up trouble, most like." John gestured toward the truck hidden in his barn. "I expect you know more than you'd like to say about troublemakers from Charlotte."

"I try to steer clear of them," Kevin said.

The farmer wheezed a laugh. "Our closest neighbor was at market last night selling produce. Claimed some big fella knocked half a dozen militia boys for a loop, stole their weapons, got clean away. You know anything about that?"

"If he did," Pablo said, "it would be foolish to discuss it."

The farmer laughed again. "We're all pals here, right?"

"Sure thing," Kevin said. "And we're grateful for your hospitality."

"And the bread," Irene said. "And cheese. And utensils."

Kevin returned to the main point. "Did your neighbor say anything about why the Charlotte militia ventured this far south?"

"Not a thing worth repeating. Got our own troops swarming like angry hornets, I can tell you that much."

Pablo asked, "Which direction?"

"North by east is what I heard." The farmer avoided meeting their eyes by kicking at the dust. "When do you aim on heading out?"

"We had thought today," Pablo replied.

"Tomorrow's better. Big rain coming in this evening. First summer storm of the season." As if in confirmation, there was a faint rumble against the clear blue sky. "There you go, now. Storm's near 'bout close enough to touch. Plus our own patrols are out in force just now. You best wait for things to settle down."

Kevin offered his hand and tried to put some feeling into his response. "Thank you very much, John."

The farmer retreated, saying, "The wife's making up a batch of crackling bread. It'll go right nice with that stew of yours."

Soon as the farmer moved off, Irene said, "What he said about the Atlanta militia. That was a lie."

Carla offered, "Forrest says no one is coming our way. But there's a lot of traffic out on the main roads. And guns."

"Tell the team to pack their gear," Kevin said. "We eat and we load and we drive."

Hamlin Turner could not see them until the early evening, which might have troubled Caleb and the others a great deal. Except for how his secretary, a tightly composed woman named Esther with the stern determination of a seasoned elder, assured them that her boss turned down twenty requests for every new client he took on. She personally escorted them to the main exit, shook their hands, and warned them to be on time.

Caleb suggested they use the hours to scout the university area. They asked directions from two young men carrying books and deep in passionate conversation. Caleb envied them their ability to stay blind to the day's risks and the world's burdens. He wished he could have known such a time himself, when knowledge was as vital as food, and the world held a heady mix of opportunity and challenge. Rather than life-or-death decisions and the very real risk that he placed friends in lethal peril with his every move.

They did their best to stroll casually through town. Caleb played the newcomer with time and money on his hands, here to do a little business, speak with his attorney, see the sights. He was young for someone with that kind of wealth, but Atlanta was the largest commercial hub south of Charlotte. There were bound to be at least a few wealthy families who sent their sons in to take care of business and enjoy everything the big city had to offer.

Caleb found Atlanta both hotter and more humid than Catawba. He did not think it was merely his own sense of oppressive urgency. Springtime in the Catawba enclave was spiced with cool dawn breezes and the frigid bite of diving into deep granite springs, with waterfalls clinging to wet rocks and the shouts of boyhood laughter ringing off the high stone walls. Caleb did not much care for this city or its close-wrapped humid heat.

No hint of wind touched the banners marking the university's guard towers. The wall surrounding the campus was a living hedge taller than the roof to Caleb's home and, according to a student they met, was almost twenty feet thick. She told them, "The Atlanta authorities claim it's to keep the students safe from all the recent immigrants. But we know better. Long before the human tide shifted this way, the barrier was up and the university gates were well guarded."

The student's name was Enya, and she and Hester were already fast friends. They had met while waiting for a table to open at a student tavern. The gates were fronted by a broad plaza lined with any number of shops catering to the students and their masters.

Enya was tall and dark-haired, and heavyset in the manner of a woman of vast appetites. Her emotions shone bright as her flashing dark eyes. "I am a student of American culture, which makes me a threat in the eyes of the local leaders. Not that I care a whit."

A young waiter called Enya's name and waved them to a table by the tavern's front wall, which meant the canopy offered them shade. Several customers ahead of them in line protested volubly, but Enya pretended not to hear as she led them through the crowded din.

Once they were settled, Caleb asked, "Why a threat?"

"Because so much of what today's leaders want us to accept as historical fact is nothing more than convenient lies." She had a quick word with the hovering waiter, who clearly wanted more from Enya than her meal order. When he departed, she went on, "After the Great Crash, a number of political groups tried to maintain unity within our nation. I know because I have seen the historical documents. They fought against the regional power grabs, and they lost. Now we live in a series of medieval fiefdoms, little better than serfs, while these so-called mayors and their cohorts squabble over wealth and power and land."

Caleb found the history lesson mildly interesting, but he could not see how it brought them any closer to their objective. He was still wondering how to broach the subject when Hester said, "We need to contact a professor. In utter secrecy."

Enya waited while bowls of stew and rough-fired mugs of some local brew were set down before them. "Who is this professor?"

Caleb supplied, "Frederick Constance."

"I do not know that name. His field?"

"Engineering. He is a wizard with electronics."

"Then he will be highly prized. What is the message?"

"Can you get us inside the campus?"

"Impossible," Enya declared. "This time last year, perhaps. Enough money could have bought you a fake university ID. But the surge of immigrants changed all that. Passes are now electronically checked."

Hester said, "Surely visitors can enter."

"With proper notice, of course. Which means either a professor or a student must make a formal application. In advance."

"Time is crucial," Hester said. "Every day counts."

"Every hour," Caleb added.

"Then you must trust me. Or not." Enya said no more while they finished their meals.

Heart in his throat, Caleb said, "The professor's daughter is missing."

Enya blanched, but conscious of surrounding eyes, she recovered as best she could. She whispered, "The militia?"

"We do not know. But I think yes."

"Why?"

"To explain would be to put you in great danger," Caleb replied.

"That sounds well enough. And your message?"

He searched the others' gazes and saw only trust. "My name is Caleb. I am here. And I can help."

"The professor will no doubt want to know why he should believe you," Enya said. "One small individual."

"Not so small," Zeke replied. "And not just one."

"One, three, big, little, you still face the strongest militia south of Washington." Enya searched their faces. "Truly, this is not just words?"

"We are staying at the Ritz," Caleb said. He saw the meaning register in Enya's gaze. "We are more than mere students, and by sharing this we place our lives in your hands."

While Kevin's team finished their meal, Pablo resumed his role as sergeant of his company. He was everywhere at once, quietly supervising those who loaded the truck while keeping Tula, Hank, and Forrest all on careful sentry. Hank was a slender waif in his early twenties, with a teen's body and an ancient's gaze. He crouched in the barn's afternoon shadows and tossed rocks while staring at the northern woods.

The farmer and his wife took up station by their kitchen door and watched them through the screen. But they made no protest, not even when Carla and Doris returned the hamper and dirty plates, nor when Kevin deposited a pile of silver coins on the stoop and said they were taking the cooking pot and wooden ladle.

They drove away in midafternoon. The truck was silent,

the sentries watchful. They headed back east as though they intended to rejoin the Augusta–Jacksonville highway. It was the logical course, for this was the nearest route that might keep them clear of Atlanta's border patrol. But five miles later, Kevin turned onto a rutted asphalt track that pointed straight south. The road was in such bad shape their progress remained little more than a crawl. He was burning fuel at a prodigious rate, but their vehicle had left Charlotte with a full tank, more than enough to make it to Atlanta and back.

They followed the asphalt trail for almost two hours. Six times their sentries raised the alert when Atlanta's militia rode nearby. But none of the hunters turned down this particular trail. Eventually Pablo ordered the sentries to refocus. They were frightening the little ones, he told the trio. The only militia that concerned them now were those who came close enough to take aim. After that, the sentries remained silent.

Finally, as the sun touched the western treetops, they found what Kevin had been hunting. Their trail ended at a T-junction, joining with a better road that ran west to east. If they took the right-hand turn they would be aimed straight for Atlanta. Kevin reversed back a quarter mile, then told the crew they could climb down and unlimber, just stay quiet. He and Pablo crept back and positioned themselves where they could observe the intersection and remain unseen.

The clouds slowly gathered and blanketed the sunset. Half an hour later, five farm carts rolled slowly by, heading away from Atlanta. Adults sat on the front benches while children sat atop burlap sacks or rode the backs of weary horses. A trio of bonnet-clad girls sat in the rearmost wagon, clapping hands and singing as they rode. Kevin saw guns in all the wagons, but none of the riders appeared to be on high alert. He assumed these families had taken wagonloads of produce into Atlanta and were now returning home with store-bought supplies. Which was why he had stationed himself here, to be certain the western road connected to a working checkpoint.

When the last wagon vanished in the eastern shadows, he rose and said, "Let's make camp."

Pablo found a clearing surrounded by a growth of new elms, with a small but clear-running stream. Once the truck was stationed for the night, Pablo went back and covered their wheel tracks off the trail. They debated, then decided they could not risk a fire.

The rain did not come that night, which was good, for they had no camping equipment. The balmy weather meant most of the team could spread out over the clearing and get a good night's rest. Kevin sat with Forrest for the pre-dawn watch. They were stationed in the truck's cab. Kevin could see nothing of the night beyond the first line of trees. Nor did he need to. He was there to ensure Forrest remained awake and attentive.

"Is it okay if we talk?" Kevin asked. "I don't want to interrupt you or anything."

"Do you stop listening when we talk?"

"Not if I'm alert."

"There you go."

Through his open window, Kevin heard the distant rumble of thunder. Somewhere beyond the thick blanket of clouds, dawn was breaking. The surrounding trees were indistinct drawings painted in shades of slate and brown. "So what's your story?"

"I was a waste-disposal engineer. Basically I loved and hated my life in equal measure. It was as safe as it was boring."

"You lived in Charlotte?"

"All my life."

"When did you discover this sensitivity of yours?"

"I was twelve." Forrest settled more deeply into his seat. "You've known other adepts?"

"Two friends. One is a hunter. The other . . . To tell the truth, I'm not sure exactly what Caleb is."

"He may not know either." Forrest waved at the slumbering forms in the clearing. "Some of our crew, they didn't have any idea they were gifted until all this started."

"Gifted," Kevin repeated, thinking of all the trouble and turmoil their abilities had caused.

"A few still don't know anything beyond the fact that they have shown the two attributes," Forrest said. "That's what the dark suits call the measurements they can identify with their helmets. Attributes." He was quiet a moment, then added, "They're the ones who still wake up screaming."

Kevin decided he didn't need to know what Hollis and the suits did to try to make those young adepts identify their abilities.

Forrest went on, "At first, all I knew was I could hear things others couldn't. My mother insisted I was making things up. When she finally accepted it was real, she was terrified. As long as she was alive, she wanted nothing more than for my gift to vanish." His tone was matter-of-fact, which to Kevin's mind only heightened Forrest's compacted sorrow. "My dad, he was great. He made up games and we practiced together in the garden shed. He pretended we'd set up a detective agency together. Another day we were backyard spies. Of course, he made it clear the gift had to stay our secret. But he made things bearable by giving me an outlet. One that was fun. One that made my father my best and only real friend."

Kevin searched the gradually strengthening day and wondered what it would be like to have such an ability and never speak of it. He thought of Caleb and Zeke and felt their lifelong burden more intensely than ever before.

The light was strong enough now for Kevin to see the man's sad smile. "I suppose that's how I stayed content with my life. I liked the orderliness of my job. I did something that went unnoticed but was crucial just the same. And from that safety, I kept searching the hidden and the unseen. But it cost me—I suppose it had to. I was married once, but it didn't take. I never told her about my ability. Now I think it was probably a mistake. Yet something held me back." Forrest sighed. "A year to the day after our wedding, she said she'd had enough of living with an enigma."

Through the cab's open rear window, Kevin heard the camp begin to stir. At the same time, the first raindrops tapped upon the truck's roof. He had a hundred more questions, a thousand. But all he said was, "We better start getting ready."

34

This used to be known as a doré bar." Hamlin Turner drew the gold closer to his eyes. "Means gold that's been refined at the mine head. Purity is never more than ninety percent. I'd put this at around eighty-five, which isn't bad for a backwoods operation. Not bad at all. I assume that's who you represent, yes? There used to be gold mines all through the Appalachians. You must have found a vein that wasn't played out."

Caleb did not respond. Nor was he certain the attorney expected him to say anything. The inner office was grand yet rumpled, just like the attorney seated behind the huge desk. The carpet stretched across the broad-plank floor was very old and very beautiful and looked hand-sewn. But the central section had lost its color, and the borders were badly frayed. The desk was as scuffed and hard used as the floor.

The ceiling was high and held three chandeliers of hand-blown glass. The wall opposite the trio of huge windows was lined floor to ceiling with shelves holding more books than the Catawba library. But the volumes lay in a careless, haphazard manner. More books were scattered over the office's three tables, along with a multitude of files. There was dust everywhere.

Hamlin Turner reflected his office's messy state. He was a big man, easily twice Caleb's weight, tall and big-boned enough to handle his bulk with relative ease. He rose from his leather chair and walked to a small kitchenette set in an alcove behind his desk. "Coffee?"

"Yes, please."

"Manners. I've always found them useful. When I can remember to use them." Hamlin inspected a mug, his fingers too big to fit inside the handle. He used a dishrag to wipe the interior. "Esther—that's the battle-ax guarding my outer office—she hates how I won't let her clean in here. But if she did, I wouldn't be able to find a thing. How do you take it?"

"I haven't had coffee often enough to know."

"Milk and sugar, that's the ticket. Makes a decent meal when time's too tight to eat." Hamlin poured them both a mug, dosed them liberally, then reached across the desk. His chair creaked noisily when he reseated himself. "Where were we?"

"I have no idea." Caleb took a cautious sip. The coffee was warming and rich. He felt himself being invited to relax in unaccustomed ways. Instead, he sensed the band of tension wrapped around his chest more clearly than ever. He had been so busy, the times so intense, he had been able to ignore the burden he carried. But now, as he sat in the safety of this powerful man's office, the worries and the unanswered questions assaulted him.

"Accepting you as a client is inviting a whole passel of trouble." Hamlin's smile held a nasty edge. "So happens I like trouble. Keeps a body on their toes. Been far too smooth sailing around here lately. Bud, you got yourself a lawyer."

"Wonderful."

"Now that we've got that out of the way, what do you aim on achieving with all this gold? You understand what I'm asking, yes?"

Caleb had been pondering that very question. "This much money means power. Which I don't want."

"It doesn't matter what you want." Hamlin leaned back and planted a massive boot on the desk. "The Atlanta leaders will all be thinking that way."

"They scare me."

"They should. First thing they'll want to know is, who am I representing, and is this person a threat or an ally. Which is why representing you could place me in very real danger." If the attorney was concerned about that prospect, he did not show it. "How much gold are we talking about?"

Caleb motioned to the three cases lined up behind the desk. "There are a hundred and thirty-nine bars we brought with us. And we hope to deliver that much every three or four months."

"Like I said, trouble." But Hamlin's grin grew broader. "Mind telling me where you're from?"

Caleb hesitated, then decided the attorney needed to know that much. "Catawba enclave."

"Which means you've decided to avoid Charlotte. Smart man. And now you want me to set you up with a safe and secret haven. Consider it done. What else?"

"That's as far as I've gotten."

"Think it over and let's meet up here tomorrow. I have to be in court all morning. Noon work for you?"

"Yes." Caleb started to rise, then added, "There is one thing."

"Thought there might be."

"It's personal, though."

"Son, you're in the process of dumping a truckload of gold in my lap. Personal is not the issue."

But Caleb persisted. "The gold, that's the property of the enclave's elders. I'm just their courier and spokesman."

"And an honest one at that. They're lucky to have you. Which permits you a personal request in my book." The grin became more wolfish still. "And I'm the only voice that matters just now."

Caleb found himself liking the hard-edged lawyer. "I'm trying to locate a missing friend. Well, more than a friend."

"She's here in Atlanta?"

"She and her father came down five months ago. Her name is Madeline Constance. Goes by Maddie. Her father taught engineering at the Catawba community college, then accepted a professorship at Atlanta University."

Hamlin picked up a pen but did not make any notes. "You've asked him?"

"I'm . . . trying."

"Caleb, why don't you go ahead and tell me what you're dancing around."

"Maddie . . . is a special. Her father doesn't know."

"This just keeps getting better." Hamlin set down his pen. "You're asking me to poke a hornet's nest."

"You won't help me?"

"I didn't say that. But it has to be done quiet, you understand. Quiet takes time."

"Yes. Thank you."

"These specials have become a matter of grave interest to the local powers. They've even got themselves a high-powered group down from Washington to help out. Though 'help' might not be the proper word, given these are Washington folk." Hamlin appeared to be talking as much to himself as to Caleb. "They're rounding up these so-called specials and holding them somewhere."

"They're not so-called anything," Caleb said.

Hamlin peered at him from beneath greying eyebrows thick as shrubbery. "Point taken."

"Can you find out where they're being held?"

"Probably. But like I said, it has to be done quiet. As in, whispering down dark wells at midnight. Where are you staying?"

"The Ritz."

"Nice place. Go get yourself a decent night's rest. Looks like you could use it. Be back here at noon. I'll see what I can find."

35

Caleb returned to the plaza fronting the university entrance just as the streetlights began to glow. Their illumination was feeble at first, but still enough to cause some pedestrians to stop and watch them come alive. He was glad that he was not the only one captured by everything those lights represented. All along the darkening street, they glowed like gemstones laid upon the path to . . . where? Caleb knew what he wanted. A world where people were free to cross from city to city, to travel and explore and be who they were, without subterfuge or fear of imprisonment for the crime of being different.

As if in response to his yearnings, thunder rumbled in the distance.

Caleb did not need a glimpse beyond time's next corner to know Maddie had been arrested in a sweep for specials. She was caught in the snare of people holding power and wanting more. He was fairly certain she was alive. And not hurt. There remained a sense of being bonded with her at some level below any direct communication. He hoped he was not fooling himself. He didn't think so. In such moments of solitary contemplation, he still caught a faint assurance that she was there. Silent for reasons of her own, waiting for him.

As he entered the plaza, Caleb hoped desperately he had been right to speak openly with Hamlin Turner. He'd entrusted his fate and that of his entire community to an Atlanta lawyer. Yet he liked Hamlin. He felt better having the man on his side. And for no other reason than that, he crossed the park and entered the tavern with a light heart.

It was a shame the feeling could not have lasted a little bit longer.

Zeke and Hester were not there. Nor was Enya.

Caleb searched the outside tables, then went inside and spotted the same waiter who had flirted with Enya earlier. The man recalled Caleb, offered him a table, and took his order for food Caleb doubted he could eat.

Two and a half hours later, the others still had not arrived.

The storm continued to gather, the wind fitful and damp. The clouds massing overhead flashed and thunder growled. Finally the waiter returned and pointed at the long line of patrons seeking a table.

Lightning flickered like electric veins overhead as Caleb returned to his hotel.

···

Caleb spent a sleepless night trapped in a double blanket of fear and guilt. He should never have left his two friends in the company of an Atlanta student. What was worse, he was doubly afraid he had been wrong to trust Hamlin. Nothing he had done seemed right, starting from the terrible moment he had revealed his ability to Harshaw and his Catawba clansmen. The enclave's future lay on his shoulders like a huge grey rock.

Lightning flickered and thunder rumbled, a portent of the storm beyond the horizon. There was no escape from the fact that he had endangered the lives of everyone he held dear.

The rain arrived with the dawn. Caleb rose from his bed and showered and ordered a breakfast brought to his room. He could not bear the thought of entering that vast restaurant alone, staring at all that wasted food, and knowing the day could well mark the last time he ate anything decent. Even so, he could scarcely force himself to keep down a cup of tea. The food sat on the tray on the elegant table in the middle of his grand parlor, mocking him and all his worries.

Flash! Boom!

The lightning crashed so close to his window that the thunder exploded in that very same moment. Caleb was hammered off his feet and landed hard on the carpet. He lay there, his limbs outstretched, as he realized for the first time what it meant to truly *see*.

All his searches for truth and right actions up to this point had merely been dabblings. He had touched his toe into the sea of his own potential, then retreated. He had done what came easily. Nothing more. Now there was no longer anything to hold him back. He was stripped bare. Even his skin was gone, even his life. Now he dove in.

He saw.

Caleb stood on an open field at midnight. A vein of fire

began at his feet. Two paths opened up and raced away from him, forming a brilliant V that illuminated the empty plain. They reached the horizon at the very same moment, then exploded.

He opened his eyes and rose slowly from the carpet. He stood before the rain-streaked window, his chest heaving. His entire body shook. He listened to the thunder of his own heart and knew without the slightest doubt that he stood at just such a juncture. He could remain the man shaped by his youth. Caleb of Catawba enclave, a quiet-spoken man who did his best by all who came his way.

Or he could become something more.

There were no guarantees to accepting the position of leadership represented by this other path. Caleb saw how the tension and fears and doubts that had wrecked his night were mere shadows of what he would know in the future. If he accepted the challenge and sought to *grow*. Become a man who sought to be strong for others. To seek the right way, even through the darkest hour. To help. To serve.

It was a terrifying choice. But as he wiped his face and waited for strength to return to his limbs, Caleb knew the choice had already been made.

The first drops fell in the hour before dawn. The rain was slow in building, but the soft patter of early droplets was overlaid with a constant rumble now, promising far more to come. They were all up and washed and fed and safe in the truck by the time the storm arrived in earnest. Kevin sat in the rear hold, with Pablo across from him. Doris had worked for a transport company and could handle the truck. When gusts of wind began blowing rain into their cubby, Pablo ordered the rear flaps shut and the lanterns lit, turning the vehicle into a safe little cave. A faint mist still drifted in under the canvas ties, but they were warm and they were content, mostly. It was time.

Kevin was seated next to Forrest. The more he got to know the man, the more he liked him. Forrest was steady. He made no bones about who he was or the life he'd made for himself.

It was an engineer's ability, Kevin thought, being able to see life for what it was and go about arranging it into as comfortable a position as possible.

He asked, "How long ago did Charlotte start the sweeps?"

Forrest said, "Three, maybe four days before we got out. Perhaps five. No more than that."

Which was why they had escaped as easily as they had. The collection and imprisonment of specials had not yet become fully organized in Charlotte. Kevin recalled the argument he had seen between Hollis and the Washington suits. The treaty or whatever agreement Charlotte had made with the capital was not resting easy with some.

He told them, "I've got a lot of questions and almost no answers."

"That's the role of a good leader, seems to me," Pablo replied.

"And that's what we need to talk about. I don't think I'm the leader you seek." He held up his hand to stop their protest. "But let's leave that for a second. There's something you need to decide first."

"*We* decide," Carla corrected.

When Kevin merely kept his hand upraised, Pablo asked, "What is the question?"

"Where are we going?"

"You know the answer to that."

"We all agreed coming to Atlanta was the right move. But then what?" He pointed at Carla. "You said I would tell us. The problem is, I have no idea why we've come or what to do now that we're here."

Carla's serene confidence remained unfazed. "You don't know *yet*."

Kevin shrugged. "Now or later, I've only got one possible answer."

The team had shifted around so they were all silently involved in the discussion. Those inside the cab listened through the sliding rear window. The faces turned Kevin's way were slick with droplets blown under the cover. The canvas ties fluttered nervously, like they feared what was being discussed.

Kevin went on, "I think maybe my job was to bring you to a different leader."

Carla halted Pablo's outburst with a tap on his leg. She asked, "Who do you have in mind?"

"His name is Caleb."

"You've spoken of him before."

Pablo demanded, "What makes you think he'll know more than you?"

"He's one of you, for a start. An adept. I'm not."

Carla asked, "What is his attribute?"

Kevin turned to Forrest. "Remember the guy I mentioned this morning?"

Forrest nodded. "Who doesn't know his real ability."

"That's him. Caleb senses things—events that haven't happened. And he's a truth-teller. His girlfriend is an adept as well. Her name is Maddie, and she forged a communication between them. She moved to Atlanta when her father became a professor at the university. Then she vanished a week or so ago. Caleb lost communication with her. So he came down here looking for her."

Forrest asked, "When?"

"He left Overpass the same day I met Carla." Kevin knew he was making a mess of this, but he had no choice except to press on. "I think he's the one. The leader you're needing. Caleb is a born strategist. He works a problem better than anybody I've ever met."

Pablo looked ready to argue. But once again his outburst was silenced by Carla tapping his leg. Kevin liked that about them, how she balanced him and he trusted her. He knew a moment's yearning for someone he could rely on like that. And love.

He went on, "I've known two real leaders. I mean, the kind of people others will not just follow but trust with their lives. One was the sheriff of Overpass, the other was my mother. I think Caleb is the third of this rare breed."

"Say you're right," Carla said. "What do we do now?"

"I have no idea." It was only when Kevin wiped away the slick covering his face that he realized his hands were shaking. "I don't know where he is. Or how we can find him."

···

"No," Irene declared. "It is not possible."

Carla asked, "Shouldn't you at least try to do what Pablo suggests before you shut the door in his face?"

From her place beside Kevin, Irene gave Carla a very cool look. "Pablo wants me to communicate with somebody who isn't listening and has never mind-communicated with anyone except the woman he loves."

Forrest had shifted down one place so that Irene now sat between him and Kevin. "Maddie probably broke through the guy's barriers with that same love."

"And intimacy," Irene said. "And time. She and Caleb grew up together, didn't you tell us that?"

"Since childhood," Kevin confirmed. The longer he was in

Irene's company, the more he felt drawn to her. Despite the fact that they were bedraggled, weary, and dirty from three very hard days without proper baths, she remained a lovely and alluring figure. Heat seemed to radiate off her, defying the gusting rain that drifted through gaps in the canvas cover. Kevin knew he should be focused on the myriad of problems they faced, but just then he found a distinct pleasure in sitting there, absorbing her warmth.

"All right, I get it," Carla said.

But Irene went on anyway. "But the more important thing, to me at least, is that Caleb is *listening* for her. He is *desperate* to hear she's alive and okay."

"Enough," Carla said.

"No, no, this is good," Kevin said. "My sheriff used to say, sometimes you find the right answer by discovering what is wrong about other options. I like hearing all this."

"So do I," Pablo said. "It's drawing things into focus."

"I have no idea what abilities we have here," Kevin said. "I know I need to learn what you can and can't do, but now isn't the time."

Forrest shifted forward, leaning his elbows on his knees so he could see around Irene. "What if, just suppose . . ."

"Tell us."

"No, forget it." He leaned back. "It sounded crazy even before it came out of my mouth."

"Crazy is better than nothing," Kevin said. "What are you thinking?"

...

The distance from the hotel to Hamlin Turner's office was less than a thousand paces. Down a broad avenue, across a rectangular park fronted by elegant townhouses and offices, two blocks along a busy street fronted by elegant shops, and Caleb was there. He was sheltered beneath an umbrella the hotel supplied but still arrived with the bottom half of his trousers drenched. The rain fell in solid sheets, a veritable wall of water. The streets were turned into fast-flowing creeks. Most people he passed cringed every time the lightning flashed, which was often. As though they feared not the rain but the other possible causes for such blasts. As though they all felt vulnerable.

The second image struck just as he climbed the building's broad stone staircase. Lightning flashed close by, and in its crackling aftermath Caleb felt this new concept become branded on his mind: an eagle in full flight, carved from a far larger storm.

The thunder spoke to Caleb then, at a level far deeper than mere words. It said the present tempest assaulted all of America. Caleb's entire nation was in need of a different direction.

The eagle's image remained poised overhead, branded upon the clouds. For one brief instant Caleb watched it feed upon the lightning, drawing strength for the conflict to come. Just as he must ready himself.

When the image passed, Caleb climbed the stairs, entered the building, and stood dripping in the grand stone foyer. He had made the decision. He would do his best to grow beyond his upbringing and the enclave's comfortable existence.

He had been moving in this direction since leaving Catawba for Overpass. Even before. He knew that now. Since the moment he had stood and watched Maddie's wagon roll out of sight, he had been heading for this moment, when he would see the nation's symbol of defiance and strength emblazoned on the sky overhead and understand what it meant. Challenging the might of those who sought to oppress and enslave. Rebelling against the wrongness. Confronting the enemy. And defeating them.

37

Forrest traded places with Pablo so that he was seated directly across from Kevin. His remaining strands of hair were drenched and mashed flat to his head by the spray drifting through the canvas opening. Irene was seated next to Forrest, waiting her turn. Silent as always.

Forrest said to Kevin, "Tell me about Caleb."

"I've only known him a little over a week."

"Tell me what you can." Forrest shut his eyes and leaned back against the canvas walls. "Focus on the emotional connection. You like him, yes?"

"A great deal. More than makes sense after such a short while. But it feels like I've known him all my life."

"Good. Very good. Now tell me why."

Kevin understood what Forrest intended through the question. He sought to fashion an impossible connection by riding Kevin's emotional link to Caleb. See if it was possible to locate someone he didn't know because of this fragile bond. Kevin felt exposed talking about his feelings in front of twenty watching faces. Even so, he forced himself to open up, while the thunder and pounding rain accented his every word.

Kevin described his meeting with Mayor Silas Fleming and the dark pleasure Captain Hollis had shown. He related how Hollis had looked forward to seeing Kevin fail at identifying specials, then stringing him and his mother from the city's lampposts. Kevin relived their flight from Overpass with Gus Ferguson's help, their fear and exhaustion, then meeting Caleb and his father by the boundary stream.

He leaned back and shut his own eyes as he recalled the moment his bleak resignation had turned to a flicker of hope, when Caleb had revealed his own gift. How he had respectfully told his father that both Kevin and Abigail should be offered sanctuary. Right then. Without the elders' full approval. Kevin described how Caleb's natural authority had been matched by respect and even humility. How in the hours and days to follow, Kevin had come to like him immensely. How he admired and trusted Caleb's leadership and the way it was balanced with a very real modesty . . .

"I have him," Forrest softly declared.

Kevin crouched on a backpack that looked frosted from the misting rain. "Where is he?"

"He's sitting in an outer office." Forrest leaned against the canvas wall, his entire face creased with concentration. "He's very . . ." He shook his head. "I don't know the word. Intent. Worried, but something more."

"It's enough." Kevin pretended a confidence he did not feel. "Okay. Irene, you ready?"

In response, she slipped her hand into Forrest's. She leaned closer to him, closed her eyes, placed her other hand atop theirs, and said softly, "Show me."

For a time, the only sound in the truck was the drumming rain. Then Irene leaned back, looked at Kevin, and said, "Nothing. I can't communicate with him at all."

Forrest did not appear the least bit surprised or disappointed by the result. He opened his eyes, released Irene's hand, and wiped the gathered moisture from his face. "It felt like we were trying to burrow through a brick wall with a spoon."

Kevin wanted to punctuate the moment, show everyone who watched that he was not discouraged. He could think of nothing to say except, "Did the suits ever ask you to do something of the sort?"

Pablo's eyes turned hard as etched glass. "They did not *ask* anything."

"They were only in Charlotte for a few days before we escaped," Forrest reminded him.

"They ordered us to show them what we could do," Pablo said. "Most of us answered honestly. We did not know what they were talking about."

"Then the examinations began," Irene said. "That was their word. All we knew was, some of us left and did not return."

"So they don't have any idea," Kevin said. "They don't have a clue who we are or what we can do."

Both Irene and Forrest offered small smiles. Pablo said, "Wouldn't it be nice to surprise them."

"It would be fantastic," Kevin agreed. "Time for round two."

Again Irene took a two-fisted grip on Forrest's hand. The two of them shut their eyes, then Forrest asked, "Are you ready?"

For an instant, Kevin thought he was the one being addressed. Then Irene said, "I feel bonded to you."

"And I to you," Forrest said. He opened his eyes long enough to smile at Kevin. "Another first."

"Focus," Irene said.

Forrest closed his eyes once more. A moment passed, then, "Kevin, tell us about the telepath, Caleb's girlfriend."

"Her name is Maddie." Kevin felt the exposure of simply not knowing enough. "I've never met her."

"Tell us what you can," Forrest said.

Kevin knew the question was coming. He had, after all, helped to design this tactic. Even so, what they sought was a daunting challenge. A man with the ability to locate the unseen sought to forge a connection through Caleb to a woman none of them had met. And then Irene was to piggyback on this so as to . . .

Irene added, "Focus on the heart."

Kevin took a breath and described how Caleb looked when he talked about Maddie. He told the silent team about the sad and worried yearning that blanketed his new friend every time he spoke about . . .

Forrest broke in with, "I have her."

An instant later, Irene shrieked and spasmed so violently she fell off the bench and sprawled at Kevin's feet.

Kevin and Carla and Pablo cried together, "What's wrong?"

Irene swatted away Kevin's attempt to help her up. She cried, "We have to go *right now*!"

Caleb entered Hamlin Turner's outer office with an intense certainty that he was surrounded by friends. On the face of things, that was beyond absurd. Zeke and Hester and their one ally among the student population had vanished. He was trusting his life and the Catawba enclave's future to a complete stranger. His recent assurance had come in the middle of a massive thunderstorm, when he was blasted by images he did not fully understand. Yet as Caleb seated himself by the side wall, he felt as though a whole company of trusted allies joined him. They might be invisible. He might not even know their names. But they were there with him. Now.

Of course, it could all just be the result of having lost a night's sleep. But Caleb was certain there was more to his unseen companions than mere exhaustion.

What was more, despite his fatigue and his grainy eyes

and his aching muscles, Caleb felt something he could not name. The sensation was so odd, he needed a long moment to even give it a name.

He felt ready.

He was still coming to terms with the prospect of taking another unseen step when the next event happened.

It was only then, as he was blasted by Maddie's message, that he named the experience. *Event*. It was by far the strongest such experience he had ever known. And it carried an underlying sense of Maddie having waited days and days and days. Through dark hours filled with hopeless fear, Maddie had clung to the certainty that he would come for her. That she could trust him. With her life.

"Caleb?"

When Caleb opened his eyes and managed to refocus, he discovered Hamlin Turner bending over him, peering down in concern. "Are you all right?"

...

Kevin's team contained seven mentats of one persuasion or another. *Mentat* was their term for adepts with the ability to register some form of mental connection with others. One-third of their total was a considerable amount. It probably meant something significant. But just then Kevin could not take time to figure it out. He was far too worried about what was about to take place.

The team's mentats came in all shapes, sizes, and levels of ability. None of them had ever attempted what he proposed. And yet all seemed more than willing to try. Even Pablo showed nothing save a calm confidence that Kevin's untested idea might work.

This group's trust in his judgment was very frightening indeed.

The rain remained their friend as they drove east, toward the city's boundary fence. As they rode, Kevin tried to gain a clearer understanding of what had happened when Irene made the connection. *Bonded* was how she described it. She had bonded with a woman she had never met, and in that instant they had been granted a compass heading. Something to point toward beyond the Atlanta border. How they were to achieve it, Kevin had no idea. But listening to Irene describe the experience was settling. Her words gave him strength to hope they would receive the next piece of the puzzle once they entered the city.

Of course, that was assuming he could get them inside.

"She was waiting for me," Irene told him. "She had been waiting for days." It was the second time she had told of her experience, and she was much calmer now. She sipped from a canteen and held her gaze steady on Kevin. He had never seen eyes like hers before. They were like a dawn mist, crystal grey and yet harboring faint hints of other colors, sky blue and meadow green. He felt like he could fall into those eyes and be happy.

The entire truck focused on Irene. Doris poked her head through the cab's rear window. Now and then she retreated and passed on Irene's words to the others seated up front.

Kevin asked, "Maddie wasn't troubled by how she didn't know you?"

Irene shook her head. "She saw the connection we had made with Caleb."

"You didn't mention that before."

"Because she didn't *tell* me. You asked me what she said,

and I told you. This was different." Irene paused for another sip from the canteen. "I don't know how Maddie did it. I don't know how I saw it either. One thing I do know. That woman is *strong*."

"What other impressions did you get?"

Irene thought a long moment. The truck trundled forward, the rain drumming upon the roof. Finally she said, "I think she had been expecting all along that Caleb would bring someone to her. A real mentat."

"So she could pass on the message."

"No." Irene was definite. "She could always communicate with Caleb, you said that yourself. What she needed was knowing that Caleb had brought others."

Kevin nodded. That made sense. "A team who could free her."

"Right. Exactly. So as soon as I connected, she sent me this . . ."

"Burst, you called it," Kevin said. He was crouched in the central space, squatting on a pack, not quite touching Irene. It was the most he had ever heard her speak. He liked her voice. It carried the soft lilt of a woman born to sing.

"I've never felt anything like that. The message was layer upon layer."

"Break it down for me."

"I already have."

"Do it again. Sometimes repetition helps new things to surface."

The look she gave him made him feel as though they were alone. In that moment, the others who watched and listened did not touch them. "I bet you are a great policeman."

"Deputy sheriff," he corrected. "Tell me."

"The top layer was a map. She showed me one portion of the university campus."

"Three buildings," Kevin said. "In the northeast corner."

"One is a barracks for adepts, with cafeteria and classroom."

"A big building, you said, with a lot more room than they need."

She nodded. "The middle building was a militia barracks, with another cafeteria. The third building was dark and scary. The only thing she showed clearly about that place was how part of the ground floor was sectioned off. It held families of those who were in the first building. Her father was in there."

Hostages, Kevin knew. "Was there a fence or anything around the three buildings?"

"They're building one. It's almost finished." She smiled with her eyes only. "I didn't say that before, did I?"

"See? Tell me about the fence."

"The city's boundary wall forms one side. When it's finished, the fence will hold all three buildings and have towers at the corners."

"Dogs?"

"I didn't . . . No." She straightened. "I just thought of something. There are suits in the dark place. Six of them. And they have a name. Specialists."

"Good, this is good." Though Kevin could not see any advantage to adding Washington specialists to the list of enemies. "You said there were layers to the message."

"Underneath the map there was a message. We have to come *now*. The adepts are beginning to give up hope. She's part of a group that has tried to hide their abilities. But a breakaway group wants to protect their families and reveal what they can do."

Hiding away was why Caleb had not heard from her, Kevin knew. His respect for this woman he'd never met grew steadily. "Anything else?"

"There was a third layer under the other two." Tears formed in the edges of Irene's eyes. "She loves Caleb very, very much."

···

Caleb allowed himself to be guided by Hamlin Turner and his secretary through the broad double doors and into Hamlin's office. He nodded at their offer of coffee, though he doubted he could drink anything. Mostly he wanted to be left alone. He needed time to absorb what had just happened. Yet time was the one thing he did not have.

There were multiple layers to Maddie's mental blast. That was precisely what she had sent to him—an explosion of energy. Carried within this force was a series of images. Just like all her previous communications, but far stronger than anything they had shared before.

Binding all the images together was an emotion so intense he still resonated with its impact.

Love. Desperate, hungry, needful love. And a confidence he would come to her rescue.

Kevin's entire team was strung out and exhausted. He knew they were barely holding it together. But no one complained. Kevin found himself admiring them. Whatever they had faced back in the Charlotte compound, it had forged them into something more than a group of individuals with special abilities.

They drove east. The storm showed no sign of easing as they approached the border. Kevin had no idea where it was exactly. For that, they relied on Forrest.

Pablo drove, holding to a slow, steady pace. Every dip in the road was filled with water. Carla was seated beside Pablo. All the mentats were gathered on the rear benches to either side of Kevin. He stood leaning against the cab, watching the rain form a constant crystal curtain. The road ahead was only visible for about fifty yards. After that, everything grew pale and indistinct, including the forest and pastures to either side. The rain washed away the summer colors, leaving everything limp and grey. They saw no one else.

Finally Forrest said, "We're almost there."

Kevin asked, "How far?"

"Half a mile. Less."

Kevin leaned down and said through the cab's rear window, "Time to pull over."

Pablo slowed and crawled forward ten yards, twenty, thirty, fifty. Then he found what he sought. He reversed into a trail and halted when the truck's snout was a few feet back from the road. Then they waited.

Twenty minutes passed. Tula and Irene and Dale handed around sacks of dried fruit and nuts and their last canteens of sweetened tea.

"Here they come," Forrest said.

Ten more minutes passed before the farm wagons rolled by, almost lost to the storm. They were pulled by horses with the quiet, patient manner of animals who had made this trip any number of times under a multitude of conditions. The four wagons were piled high with produce covered by broad, dark tarps. The front benches each held two people, all of them huddled beneath tentlike slickers and wide-brimmed hats. No one glanced their way.

As the first wagon passed, Kevin said, "Irene, you ready?"

In response, she rose and stood beside him. At a gesture from Kevin, Forrest slid into her place along the bench.

Irene peered through the canvas, her gaze tight. Finally she nodded and said softly, "Jodie?"

A plump woman in her midthirties with an abundance

of unruly red hair remained seated on the bench. Her eyes were clenched shut. "I have them. Which ones do I take?"

Kevin replied, "All of them." These two mentats were assigned to all the wagon riders. But the last wagon mattered most.

The remaining five mentats were clustered together on the bench to his left. They watched him now with round, unblinking gazes. The aim was identical for everyone they encountered, wagoners and border guards alike. All of them were to receive multiple imprints. Kevin let them decide. The younger mentats turned it into a game, competing with one another to come up with their own singular image. One suggested that their truck was in fact just another farm wagon. Another that they did not exist at all. Two decided to work together, turning them into an Atlanta militia truck, returning empty after dropping off a border patrol and checking on the outer guards. In the passenger seat rode a major.

Kevin tapped on the roof. Pablo restarted the engine and pulled back onto the road. Kevin guided Irene down beside the redheaded woman and said, "Team two, you're up."

They were a scraggly, wet, and unkempt bunch. Kevin could not recall most of their names. His fear over what they were about to attempt drowned out all else.

A sudden flash of lightning illuminated the guard station. Kevin jerked as if he had been struck by the flash. They were far closer than he'd thought. The first wagon had already halted by the barrier. Pablo was clearly caught unawares, for he hissed in alarm. One by one the mentats shifted over, peered through the canvas, nodded, and were replaced by the next. The motor growled as inch by inch they drew closer to the border crossing. Lightning blasted once more, this time so close the sound and flash came as one. They all jumped.

"Steady," Kevin said, amazed at how calm he sounded. "Focus now. Everybody stay on target."

The barrier raised and the first wagon trundled through. Then the second. Up ahead a horse nickered. The blockhouse appeared as a hulking square to Kevin's left.

Everyone held their breath as the last wagon passed beneath the barrier. Carla and the four adepts huddled on the cab's rear seat appeared frozen in place. Pablo continued to crawl forward.

One of the sentries manning the barrier saluted them.

The truck accelerated.

They were through.

Hamlin Turner entered his office, shut the door, and announced, "I haven't been able to locate your friends."

Caleb acknowledged the news with a tight nod. In truth, he remained intent upon what he had just received. Maddie's many-layered message was far clearer to him than the lawyer's words.

Seemingly aware that something had rocked Caleb's world, Hamlin had left him alone in the massive inner office and seen to other affairs. An hour or more had passed—Caleb wasn't sure of time's exactitude. Long enough for him to drink two mugs of that excellent brew and to sort out most of what Maddie had sent him. Layer upon layer, including a map of where he was to strike.

The question was how.

Caleb was far less worried than logic might have demanded. The dynamics had changed now. The internal barrier of fear and doubt had been breached. In the space of one long breath, Caleb passed through all the reasons to remain locked in uncertainty. He now entered the realm of all that was yet to unfold.

Maddie's messages always arrived as a compacted group of ideas. Caleb usually took several days to sort through them, to digest them and the exquisite emotions that bound them together. This time was different. There were so many different images, they flashed like playing cards, in and out of view in split seconds. And yet each was . . . Caleb recalled a word his mother often used. *Prescient.* More than clear. Painted in vivid, electric tones.

"I've had to be extremely careful." Hamlin crossed the office and sank into the chair behind his desk. "Rule of law only protects us so far these days. Which means, if I ask the wrong person the wrong question and it gets back to the authorities, we could both wind up very dead. Or worse."

"I've found her."

"Through your friends who went missing?"

"No, they're still absent. Others are helping."

Hamlin looked genuinely worried. "You and your surviving friends really must take great care. This is no longer just about the Atlanta bosses. Washington is involved."

Caleb nodded. "Which is why I need to set up contingency plans. In case I don't survive."

Hamlin looked ready to argue, but in the end he drew out a pen and fresh sheet of paper. "What do you have in mind?"

Caleb responded with a question of his own. "What would the Atlanta authorities anticipate happening next?"

"Excuse me?"

"You said the local rulers expect someone with this much wealth to translate it into power."

"I don't follow."

"I want to set up a smoke screen. Give them what they expect to find."

"I don't . . . You were talking about contingencies."

"Whatever happens to me, this is what I want you to do."

"What about your missing friend, the woman whose father—"

"Maddie is more than a friend. Call her my fiancée." That was a stretch, since Caleb first had to locate her and rescue her, then ask her to marry him. But still.

"So . . ."

"When people ask about the gold, and they will, tell them you represent a group seeking to forge new alliances. With Atlanta and Washington both. And you'll only identify who we are once these alliances are in place."

Hamlin frowned. "Am I correct in guessing this is not your true aim?"

"Peace is. Absolutely. But not like they expect."

"I don't understand."

"You will." Caleb could feel the press of events pushing him onward. This contact was no longer an end in itself. It was merely one step forward. And he could feel himself being pressed to accelerate. "Can you turn the bars into gold coins?"

"Can I . . ." Hamlin clearly disliked how he was no longer in control of the dialogue. "I suppose, yes. It's certainly possible. But . . ."

Caleb stood and reached across the desk for pen and paper. The image he had received just before entering the lawyer's building made sense now. It fit together with the dawn impressions and Maddie's message like pieces of different puzzles that only made sense when re-created into one unified structure.

He swiftly drew the design he had seen imprinted in the rain. "Make them half-ounce coins. On one side print this."

Hamlin rose and turned his head to study the drawing. "It looks like a revised symbol of the American eagle."

"Right. That's what they're to be called. Eagles."

"And on the coin's other side?"

"Alternate words. Freedom. Unity. Peace. Democracy."

Hamlin took the pen and wrote on the paper bearing the symbol. "Rule of law."

"Good."

"Declaration of Independence. One man, one vote."

"You decide." Caleb wished he could dwell on the moment, for the sensation that accompanied the discussion was . . . exquisite. But there was no time. "I need a way to communicate with you. Where we can be certain no one else will hear what we discuss."

Hamlin straightened and studied him a long moment. "Such a thing, if it existed, would be extremely expensive and highly illegal."

Caleb just waited.

Hamlin must have seen what he wanted, for he seated himself and reached into his bottom-right drawer. He drew out a bulky apparatus, about twice the size of a gold bar. "This is called a satellite phone. It works on the basis of technology from before the Great Crash." He pointed at the ceiling. "High overhead are . . . Never mind. What you need to know is this. It only works between midnight and three o'clock in the morning, when the last functioning satellite is directly overhead."

Caleb forced himself to concentrate as Hamlin showed him how to use the phone, then accepted an extra battery pack and instructions on how to charge them. Hamlin assured him the two batteries were fully charged and would stay good for many hours of conversation.

Caleb wrote down the number for Hamlin's own device, stowed it all in his backpack, and said, "Whoever else comes with more gold bars, tell them of this conversation. Ask them to treat what we have just discussed as my dying wish."

Hamlin's features crumpled with the effort to maintain control. "I dislike such farewells intensely."

"Let's hope this isn't one." Caleb offered the lawyer his hand. "I have to go."

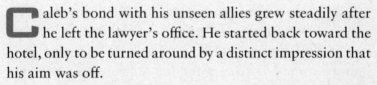

aleb's bond with his unseen allies grew steadily after he left the lawyer's office. He started back toward the hotel, only to be turned around by a distinct impression that his aim was off.

The sleepless night had left him disoriented, as if his feet had trouble connecting to the wet sidewalk. A light rain still fell, the droplets so fine they drifted in the air before his face. The wind had died while he was inside with Hamlin. The drifting mist clung to every surface. Caleb smelled fresh-baked bread and grilling meat from some nearby restaurant. He breathed in and out, hunting. He sensed a delicate presence, one he could not name. Not Maddie. Of that he was certain. Someone else.

Caleb stepped back until he met the office building's stone facade. The thoroughfare was busy at midmorning with any number of vehicles, mostly horse drawn but some motorized. Pedestrians passed him with faces shielded by umbrellas or slickers. No one paid any mind to the young man idling by the building's front steps, becoming drenched in the drifting rain.

Then Caleb's vague sensations coagulated. The grey light and the mist grew denser, more defined. The hairs on the back of his neck rose as a shadow took form in the rain, standing there directly in front of his face. It was indistinct at first but gradually took on form and clarity.

Caleb asked, "Who are you?"

■■■

Kevin and his team were scarcely a mile inside the Atlanta boundary fence, going extremely slow as a bevy of farm wagons and herds of cattle blocked all but one lane of the road. No one else seemed the least bit interested in hurrying anywhere. They joined a long line of vehicles threading their way through the rain-swept havoc that framed the city's main produce market. They could hear the cries of animals and the shouts of drovers and the calls of merchants over the engine's constant growl.

Finally they were past and just beginning to accelerate. Kevin had no idea where they were going, only that soon they would need to dump the truck and continue on foot. But where?

As he leaned down to ask Pablo that very question, Irene shrilled, "*Stop!*"

Pablo hit the brakes so hard they all tumbled about. Behind them, a wagon driver shouted angrily. Pablo restarted the engine and pulled to one side of the road. "What just happened?"

"Shush!"

Kevin pulled himself up from the jumble of packs and bodies and stared down at Irene. She appeared unaware that she lay sprawled atop Forrest.

Kevin offered her a hand up, but she did not seem capable of seeing, though her eyes were round and staring. He reached down and, with Forrest's help, levered her to a sitting position on the bench. Irene gave no sign she even noticed. She stared blindly at the canvas top. Pablo cut the engine. The only sound was the soft patter of rain and the swish of traffic beyond their vehicle.

Irene continued to search with sightless eyes, then she called softly, "Caleb?"

Indistinct was the word Irene used to describe her communication with Caleb. Like trying to hear someone standing at a distance and shouting through a heavy storm. Even so, she emerged from that first connection knowing their destination. A tavern on the square fronting the university entrance.

They abandoned the truck in the chaos surrounding the city's central market. People streamed about them, a steady flow with most faces covered against the rain. Kevin's team unloaded and hefted their packs and started off. Three times he stopped at food stalls, buying meals for those who were hungry and asking directions. No one showed more than a passing interest.

It took them almost two hours to reach the square, long enough for the youngest and weakest to be groaning softly from carrying their sodden packs. Even Kevin was shivering from the rain. But he did not mind, for up ahead was his friend and, even more important, answers.

When they arrived, Caleb was there to greet them. Kevin's gold secured them two comfortable chambers overlooking a tree-lined square and the university gates. They enjoyed a very fine meal of stew and fresh-baked bread and cheese and clay pitchers of lemonade spiced with honey from the inn's own hives.

Eventually the last of the crew emerged from the showers. By sharing what they had, everyone wore dry clothing. The beds were covered with inert bodies, some sleeping, others propped up against stacks of pillows. Those who were awake watched Kevin and Pablo and Caleb intently. They might not fully understand what was at stake. But they could sense things. Kevin had noticed this about them. Small elements that, when woven together in such quiet reflective moments as this, revealed abilities that were not yet fully understood. One of these elements was how Kevin remained busy redefining the word *team*.

As though in response to Kevin's thoughts, Caleb asked, "Tell me what you can do."

Pablo replied, "Most of us only have a faint inkling of what might be possible."

Caleb was seated in the chambers' best chair. Pablo had drawn it away from the writing desk and positioned it near where Kevin stood, facing the main room and the double doors. Everyone could see Caleb clearly as he nodded his understanding. "You have survived this long by hiding. You've never had a chance to test your boundaries."

Carla said, "This is as true for you as for any of us, yes?"

Caleb nodded again. "The one time I showed an outsider

what I could do, I risked the safety of everyone and everything I hold dear. How did you find me and Maddie?"

"It was Kevin's idea," Carla said.

Pablo pointed to Forrest. "He found you, then tracked Maddie through that connection. Irene—that's her over there—she tried to communicate directly."

Irene spoke for the first time since Caleb had joined them. "Shouldn't I try to tell Maddie we're coming?"

"Not until we know the how and the when," Caleb replied.

"But she's so *frightened*."

"I don't think fear is the right word to describe what she sent our way," Caleb replied.

"She's scared, sure," Forrest agreed. "But her urgent need for secrecy was louder."

Caleb added, "Maddie sent us that layered burst because they are being monitored."

"Layered burst," Forrest said. "I like that."

"We need to wait," Caleb repeated.

"We can't let anyone know we're coming until we're there," Pablo agreed.

Caleb went on, "The question now is, how do we rescue them? It's not enough to break them out."

"If it was just about exploding a few walls, they'd already be gone by now," Kevin said.

"I've been wondering about that too," Pablo said.

"Freeing them from their prison is only step one."

"And their families," Forrest added.

"Stopping the militia from attacking us once they're out and we've joined up, that's two," Pablo said.

"Breaking back through the Atlanta border fence, that's three," Kevin said.

"Stopping them from following us, four." This from Hank, who was sprawled on the nearest bed and addressed his words to the ceiling.

"Which means we need more transport," Kevin said.

"All this leads us to the biggest issue of all," Caleb said. This time no one spoke.

Caleb gave that a long moment, then said, "Where are we going? We need to decide that now. Because once we start moving, there won't be a chance for further discussion. After we leave this room, speed will be our only friend."

More of those lying atop the beds sat up. Several of those in the other room moved forward until they filled the doorway.

"Where can we find a safe haven?" Caleb looked around the room. "That needs to be our goal. A place where we can live and make choices for ourselves. And for all the other specials—"

"Adepts," Pablo said.

"Adepts. That's good. I like that."

Kevin said, "You have an idea, don't you."

"I think so," Caleb replied. "Half of one, anyway."

Carla asked, "Did you have a far-seeing?"

Caleb leaned back in his chair. "I like that too. Far-seeing."

"Did you?"

"Yes."

"Will you tell us?"

"Yes," Caleb replied. "I'll tell you everything."

* * *

The rain had stopped by the time they left the inn and headed for the university's main gate. The sky remained veiled by thick clouds, and the air was very close and humid.

Caleb sweated in the heat and worried over having so little to do. He found it hard to observe as others decided their fate. And up ahead, beyond the tall green barrier, Maddie waited.

"Steady," Kevin said calmly. "Everyone just walk forward at your normal pace."

"Pay attention to the man," Pablo added. "We all belong. Or we should. And we will, soon as our mentats do their little job on these fellows up ahead."

Caleb liked Kevin immensely and was coming to hold the same affection for the former militia sergeant, Pablo. As they approached the sentries manning the university gates, Caleb realized he had not seen Kevin limp once since they had met up. But now was not the time to ask, for right then Kevin said softly, "Everybody on target. Ready?"

"We are so far beyond ready," Pablo replied. "We've been waiting for this all our lives."

"Okay," Kevin said. "One, two, three. Insert."

That was the word the scraggly-haired man named Forrest had suggested. The mentats inserted mental images into the group of six guards, three by the gatehouse and three to either side of the barrier. They *blanketed* the group.

The six militia slumped as though caught in a somnolent web.

Kevin walked at the front of the group. He showed the lead guard an empty sheet of paper. Caleb doubted the soldier saw anything. The guard waved to his mates, and in response they silently raised the barrier. Caleb passed close enough to the senior trooper to touch him. Any question he might have had about the power of his team vanished with that one brief glimpse into those blank, unseeing eyes.

Inside the barrier, Caleb was tempted to pause and take

stock. Most of the buildings he could see were uniform in design, red-brick and three stories and fronted by patios and numerous whitewashed pillars. They stood upon a lawn of emerald green, with ancient oaks lining the quiet lanes. It was a place of carefully guarded peace, except for what lay directly ahead of them.

Fifty paces inside the barrier, the lane ended in a T-junction. On the intersection's other side rose the militia headquarters.

The Atlanta flag hung damp and defeated by the sultry day. The bottom floor was lined by four broad whitewashed garage doors. The three open doors revealed a pair of gleaming troop carriers and what could only have been a fire engine.

Pablo called softly, "Everyone keep moving. Don't cluster. Caleb, which way?"

The map was clear in Caleb's head. "We follow the street around to the left." Then an idea took form. He slowed and studied the militia's building.

Two guards, a man and a woman, stood just inside the central portal. They smoked cigarettes and watched the group's passage with bored expressions. The woman spoke softly. The man laughed, then flicked his cigarette in a high spiral. It landed at Caleb's feet and died with a hiss.

The man's contempt added a further spark to Caleb's idea. He waited until they had rounded a bend in the road, then said, "Let's stop here a second."

"Why?" Carla asked.

"Because we need transport."

Kevin offered a wolfish grin. "I've been wondering the same thing."

Pablo looked the most eager of all. "That makes three of us."

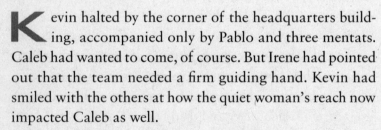

Kevin halted by the corner of the headquarters building, accompanied only by Pablo and three mentats. Caleb had wanted to come, of course. But Irene had pointed out that the team needed a firm guiding hand. Kevin had smiled with the others at how the quiet woman's reach now impacted Caleb as well.

At a gesture from Pablo, the three mentats stopped and stood shoulder to shoulder. Kevin told them, "Our goal is to rescue the Atlanta adepts."

"And their families," Pablo added. "And to do that, we need those trucks."

Kevin liked how he and Pablo were working in sync. Two sergeants, comfortable with frontline action, trusting their leader to point them in the right direction. He asked, "Ready?" At a nod from the trio, he said, "Okay. Blanket them."

Kevin approached the red-brick building with his heart in his mouth. The building was massive and as uncaring as the two guards who watched him. The man who had flicked his cigarette at Caleb said to the woman, "What did I tell you? These students, it's something all the time."

The woman started to reply, but at that instant her face went from edgy and stern to utterly blank. Kevin found his nerves settling as a result.

He walked up to the guardsman, moving in very close because he wanted to make sure the man had experienced the same effect. "We've been ordered to requisition two trucks."

The man appeared to inspect the same blank paper Kevin had shown at the gate. But his eyes were unfocused and his expression as slack as the woman's. The guard showed no interest in taking the paper. "Sure thing."

"Fetch me the keys," Kevin said. He stuffed the paper into his pocket, or tried to, but it was so wet by then it ripped into pieces. If the guards even noticed, they gave no sign.

The male guard was already moving. "Right away."

Pablo said to the woman, "Open the other door, please."

The woman turned silently away.

As Kevin walked around to the driver's door of the first truck, two other guards clattered down metal stairs at the garage's rear. They appeared as helplessly trapped in the mentats' work as the first pair.

Kevin accepted both sets of keys, tossed one to Pablo, and told the newcomers, "Go back upstairs."

The two turned and complied.

Kevin cast a swift look at the grinning Pablo, but before he could speak, everything fell apart.

A boxy black vehicle jammed on its brakes directly in front of the headquarters' driveway. A dark-suited woman wearing the bulky headset leaned out the side window and screamed, "Sound the alarm! Arrest those abominations!"

Kevin leapt into the cab, fired the engine, and did the only thing that came to mind. He raced the motor to red-line, slapped the gearshift into reverse, and roared out of the garage.

Straight at the vehicle and the Washington suits barring their way.

He slammed into the car so hard it rocked up on two wheels, groaned in time to the cries from inside, and fell over on its side. Still Kevin pushed, his own tires burning hot and the massive truck shuddering with the effort. The Washington vehicle groaned louder still and rolled over on its back.

The dark-suited woman sprawled in the grass, yelling something that was lost to Kevin's engine. Her helmet was spilled onto the drive and was shattered when Pablo's truck ran it over. She rolled away, still screaming.

Kevin halted for the three gawping mentats. As the trio clambered on board, the alarm by the gatehouse started clanging.

aleb leapt into the first vehicle's cab while the others piled into the rears of both vehicles. Pablo shouted something through the second cab's open window, his words mangled by the hooting alarm, but his message still clear. *Hurry!*

Kevin flashed Caleb a swift grin, as though it was all great fun, then reached over and helped Irene cram herself into the seat next to Caleb. Gradually the gatehouse alarm faded as they drove.

Kevin asked, "Where to?"

"Straight! Straight!" Caleb's racing heart and the grinding motor and the faint shouts from militia guards and the alarm all made it difficult to think. But the map contained in Maddie's last image was still clear before his eyes.

Kevin raced down the street, scattering pedestrians and cyclists alike. Then a trio of militia ran out from one building, waving their arms and shouting. Kevin gave the horn a cheery beep and took aim. They leapt aside at the very last minute, as though unable to believe someone would actually defy their authority. Kevin and Irene both laughed out loud.

"Left!" Caleb shouted. "Turn left!"

The truck shot around the corner so fast it reared up on two wheels, then bounced down hard. The steering wheel skittered beneath Kevin's hands like the reins of a nervous horse. He fought for control, slapped the gearshift, and accelerated.

Caleb could not believe his ears. The man was actually humming. "What has gotten into you?"

"I always get like this before going into action."

Caleb wanted to tell him how insane that sounded, but Irene chose that moment to say, "Maddie says to tell you she's ready."

The woman's calm was as jarring as Kevin's bouncy tune. "She knows?"

"We've been talking since the alarm started." Irene clutched for a handhold as the truck swept around a sharp bend. "There's no longer any need for secrecy."

"But . . . Those buildings!" Caleb pointed down a long, empty road to a trio of structures standing by themselves. "That's them!"

A trench had been started, and massive earth-moving machinery glistened in the dank grey light. The unfinished boundary fence formed an arc around the left-hand building, stretching back to where it met with the taller city wall. The buildings themselves were smallish, only two stories, with no windows on the ground floor. They appeared as blankly hostile as the militia barracks.

The earth gleamed a rich red where it had been dug up and reshaped into a curved mound, almost as tall as a man. Atop this rose a series of metal staves, thick as young trees. Bales of barbed wire lay in the grass in front of the mound. There were no vehicles along this road, or cyclists or idling groups of students. Nor was there any need of warning signs. The unfinished barricade said it all.

As Kevin raced down the empty lane, the door to the central building opened and a mass of troops spilled out. Forrest leaned through the rear window and shouted, "Suits! Suits!"

"I see them." Kevin slowed only slightly, then turned the wheel and steered the truck through a wide arc until it faced the road. He yelled, "Mentats!"

Caleb was fearful of how exposed they all were. Relying on untrained mentats seemed ludicrous, but he had no better idea. He opened the truck door and spilled onto the pavement because he refused to take his eyes off the militia clambering up the embankment, settling into protected positions, and taking aim . . .

"Guns!" Forrest's voice had risen to that of a young girl's. "They're taking aim at—"

The dismal, overcast day was shattered by a scream.

It was unlike anything Caleb had ever known or even thought might exist. The scream was in fact made from no sound at all. Instead, it emanated from every surface. The grass shimmered in time to the high-pitched shriek. The air crystallized and reknit and blasted apart. Over and over and over, until Caleb was certain his brain would shatter as well.

Then silence.

He found himself curled into a tight little ball on the wet asphalt. He lifted his head to find Kevin sprawled half inside and half outside the truck. Irene lay beside him, her hands clamped to either side of her head. From the truck's rear cabin came the sound of wails and weeping.

Kevin groaned, "What . . ."

Between the two trucks and the barricade, Pablo walked alone. His arms were extended slightly to either side of his body. He moved very slowly, approaching the barricade like he was offering himself as a sacrifice. Only there was no one to accept his surrender. The troopers and suits writhed on the muddy bank.

Caleb forced himself to stand, and in that instant he realized that Pablo was causing the strident scream. The mental noise was pointed forward. As Pablo passed, so too did the chaotic din.

Caleb shouted, "Everybody come with me!" He did not recognize his own voice. His throat felt constricted from the impact of Pablo's attack. His limbs rebelled against the need to carry his weight forward. Still he moved. "Kevin!"

"Here." The man gasped and staggered, but he came.

"Everyone! Help us!"

Caleb did not turn to see who came. He heard footsteps. How many, he had no idea. He accelerated until he moved just behind Pablo. The silence here was exquisite. He was sheltered behind the man's horrible aim, while ahead of him dozens upon dozens of the enemy writhed in torment. "Gather their weapons!"

Pablo continued to walk forward, which meant the first line of the enemy was now behind them. They had been impacted by the assault far longer than Caleb, and none of them could focus or bring their limbs under control. Yet.

The barricade hill was a mass of slippery mud. Caleb found it easier to reach up and grab an ankle or arm and haul the groaning, weeping soldiers and suits down to where he could strip away their guns. He searched them as quickly as he could, tossing everything into a growing pile on the lawn behind them. More and more of his team joined in until the weaponry was waist high and still growing.

Caleb reached the end of the gathering just as Pablo turned around. Their gazes met across the expanse of mud and moat and groaning men. Pablo offered him a fierce grin. For the first time in his life, Caleb understood what it meant to be a warrior on attack, the adrenaline rush that overcame all fear.

He yelled, "Mentats!"

A young voice turned younger still by everything that was happening called back, "Here!"

"Tell the enemy to run for their lives!"

The suits and militia staggered to their feet and fled. Then the door to the left-hand building burst open. Six suits and twice as many militia poured out, their faces stretched taut in terror. Still more stumbled from the central building. They were joined by another group from the third structure, a veritable flood of panic-stricken troopers. Two of them passed so close to Caleb he heard their wheezing gasps for breath they could not find. Their eyes were glazed with tears. They clawed the air as they stumbled and crawled and wept and fled.

Far in the distance, the alarm continued to wail.

Then they were alone, just a clutch of mud-streaked and bedraggled adepts, staring wondrously at the fleeing mob.

"Caleb!"

He whirled about as Maddie stepped through the portal, leapt down the stairs, and flew into his arms.

45

Caleb found it wrenchingly hard to let go of Maddie's hand. They only had time for one long, strong embrace and a few words spoken in such a rush he did not actually remember what he said. Or how she responded. They stood between the truck and the middle building's entrance and held hands for just a few short moments. Then Pablo called to him, and he had to let go.

Even so, their bond remained after their hands parted and she was no longer standing next to him. The sensation of her closeness was that intense.

There were a hundred things that required his urgent attention. Maddie's group totaled thirty-seven adepts plus twice that many family members. About half those adepts were under ten years of age. They would never fit everyone into the two trucks.

Just as the families started pouring from the middle building, two truckloads of militia careened around the far corner and entered the otherwise empty lane.

Kevin shouted, "Pablo!"

Pablo had already stepped forward. The first truck slammed into the curb and then was struck from behind by the second vehicle. None of the occupants appeared to notice, however. They were too busy yelling and shrieking and spilling from every opening.

Pablo stopped and turned and waved to Kevin, who yelled a second time, "Mentats! Tell them to flee!"

The enemy did as they were told.

Caleb was grateful for how the others seemed to know what to do. Carla and Irene and Forrest served as a calming influence upon the tearful reunions that now filled the front lawn. Families were given a moment to embrace, to cry, to call to friends, and then were sent back indoors to pack. Only what they could carry, Caleb repeated over and over, his words carried by a dozen more voices.

Then Zeke stepped through the left-hand building. He offered Caleb a single wave before rushing over and embracing Hester. The young man's reserve was gone now, stripped away by whatever had happened to them. The two made room for Enya when she appeared, then the trio walked over together.

Zeke said, "Sorry to have let you down."

Caleb shook his head. He wanted to say something, offer assurance that this was the absolute last thing he felt. But Carla and Hank and three others asked if there was time to fashion a quick meal. He scanned the perimeter, saw how Forrest had three of his fellow adepts guarding the empty lane, and said, "Hurry."

Hester then told Caleb, "We were arrested."

Enya said, "The suits made a sweep of the plaza just after you left. They picked up Zeke."

"I wanted to fight," Zeke said. "I started to. But . . ."

"I told him not to," Hester said. "There were militia by the university gates not twenty paces away. There was too much risk of harming others."

"First thing they did was separate us," Zeke said. "I knew you were coming. So I waited."

Caleb struggled to fashion a decent reply but was halted from speaking at all by Maddie walking up, nodding a solemn hello to Zeke, and saying, "There's my father."

Caleb heard the sorrow and resignation in more than just her words. Maddie made no move to hold his hand again. Nor did she step toward the tousled man who peered confusedly about him. When he spotted Maddie, he hesitated a long moment. It seemed to Caleb that he started toward them with genuine reluctance.

At a nudge from Hester, the trio stepped away.

To Caleb's eyes, Professor Frederick Constance appeared to have aged twenty years in the weeks since they had last met. He asked his daughter, "You arranged this escape?"

"Yes, Father. We all did."

"You said you would." He peered at Caleb. "I know you. You're . . ."

"Caleb," Maddie said. "He came for me. For all of us."

The professor tried to straighten from his weary stoop, but failed. He was leaning over so far the spectacles tied about his neck with a piece of string dangled like a loose necktie. "You can't possibly expect to break free."

"You don't need to come with us. I wish you would, but . . ."

Maddie sounded sorrowfully resigned. "But if you're staying, you should probably be leaving now."

The professor looked askance at them both. "They will destroy you!"

"I will not be imprisoned," Maddie said. The way she spoke, Caleb was certain she had said the words many times before. "I will not be manipulated. I will not be used as an instrument of someone else's civil war."

Professor Constance glared at Caleb, or tried to, but even his gaze lacked sufficient heat. "You're one of them too. One of those—"

"Adepts," Caleb supplied. "Yes. I am."

The man dismissed Caleb with a boneless wave. He turned back to his daughter. "Maddie, it's utterly futile to even think—"

"Goodbye, Father. I will send word when I can."

The rest of his protest died unspoken. The professor sighed and shuffled away, headed down the empty lane.

Maddie did not watch him go. She wiped her face, took a hard breath, and dismissed the episode by saying to Caleb, "I knew you'd come. And I knew he'd stay. He would never accept me as one of the . . ."

"Adepts," he repeated.

Maddie nodded, taking the word in deep. "Perhaps if Mother were still alive. But Father has always been . . ."

She went quiet again because Kevin came rushing over and said, "You're Maddie."

"This is my friend Kevin," Caleb said.

"Thank you for being here," Maddie said.

Kevin showed her the same feral grin he had displayed in the truck. He said to Caleb, "We're ready to start loading. Pablo wants a word."

He nodded, accepting the fact that they were looking to him as their leader. Waiting for him to direct, point their way to safety.

It was Maddie who finally said, "I'll help with the little ones."

Caleb watched her walk away, then said to Kevin, "I'm worried they haven't counterattacked."

Kevin's grin only broadened. "You took the words right out of Pablo's mouth."

They walked over to where Pablo stood with Forrest and two mentats. Thunder growled in the east. Caleb watched a dark sheet of rain march toward them, flanked by lightning. Behind him, several voices called for the families to move faster.

A bolt smashed them all with noise and light. At that same moment, Caleb was impacted by yet another mental onslaught. Two images, both so brief they came and went in the span of a single heartbeat. They left him stunned in their aftermath, as if his vision was impaired by an overbright flash of light.

"Caleb?"

"I know what they're going to do." He also knew there was not time to explain. For even now the enemy was preparing to invade. Overwhelm. Imprison. And kill those responsible. He knew it so intensely he could feel the noose being fitted around his neck.

The rain began, a drenching downpour that blanketed those still outside the trucks.

Caleb said, "They've been waiting for us to collect in one space."

Forrest's unruly hair was plastered to his face like scraggly wires. "I don't detect—"

"They're here. They've been preparing for this." Caleb halted further discussion by stabbing one finger into Pablo's chest. "Take the ones who can attack. Climb to the roof of the farthest building." When Pablo hesitated, Caleb shoved him hard. "Go *now*!"

Pablo's entire demeanor underwent a drastic shift. He became a military subaltern who had just been handed an urgent order. He shouted for Barry, grabbed a young woman's arm, and disappeared into the veiled half-light.

Kevin demanded, "What do we do?"

Caleb shook his head. There was no protection. No time for explaining. "The one you told me about. He pushed away the highway barricade—"

Kevin turned and bellowed, "Dale!"

"Here!"

The young man looked impossibly young to entrust with seventy-odd lives. He shivered in the chilling rain and winced at each stab of lightning.

Caleb gripped his arms and moved in so close that Dale had no choice but to focus entirely on him. Caleb yelled a few terse sentences, then demanded, "Can you do that?"

To his vast relief, Dale grinned and replied, "No problem."

Caleb turned to Kevin. "Take him over to the boundary fence. *Hurry!*"

Kevin grabbed Dale where Caleb's hand had been and plucked the younger man away. As he passed Forrest, Kevin reached out his free hand and hauled him away as well.

Caleb searched in all directions. The one thing he could think of, the only action that made sense now, was . . .

"Maddie!"

"Here!"

She stood by the lead truck, handing in a sack of food. Caleb rushed up, spun her about, and embraced her with all the strength he had in his body. "I need you to know—"

But he was too late.

The counterattack began as a moan.

There was no sound, or rather, nothing that anyone actually heard. Not that it mattered. To Caleb it felt as though the entire world groaned aloud.

The power was as unrelenting as it was massive. The moan gathered force, magnifying in strength until it rendered Caleb and all the others completely helpless. He collapsed onto the road, where the rain was so heavy he could have drowned in the wash beside the truck. He felt his nostrils fill and coughed feebly and managed to turn his head slightly up into the rain. Then his strength left him entirely.

The silent lament grew stronger still.

The mental attack was a cry of utter hopelessness. Caleb's every thought was futile. He lay there with no space for anything save defeat. The easiest thing in the world was to give up entirely. Stop breathing. And perish.

Then the sound vanished.

Fast as it had arrived, it was gone. Caleb coughed and lifted his head and realized Maddie had fallen across his chest. Or perhaps her strength of will was more potent than his and she had managed to reach him before being overwhelmed. Caleb helped her rise to a seated position, then grabbed the truck's rear gate and hauled himself to his feet.

He looked back behind him and knew Pablo had reached the roof in time.

Caleb helped Maddie to her feet, gripped her in a one-armed embrace, and watched as their own assault silenced the enemy.

Lightning fell in savage force. Caleb recalled Kevin describing how they had stolen the first truck using Barry's ability to control electromagnetic force. Here was the next phase, turned into an awesome display of natural fireworks.

Though it was vital to their survival, still Caleb was held by the sheer wonder of what he witnessed. The lightning blasts were intensely brilliant, the sound deafening. And yet as the others gradually slipped from the trucks and witnessed it, none of the faces Caleb saw showed any fear.

Out where the militia trucks blocked off their lane, vehicles and buildings erupted. Debris rose in damp clouds before falling back to earth. An entire tree catapulted up above the rooflines, spiraling before disappearing once more.

The lightning stopped. It took a long moment for Caleb's ears to stop ringing. When they did, he heard faint cries and numerous alarms and horns and shouts.

Then the rain pulled away from them.

Caleb could actually see the storm being redirected. The curtain drew back, slanting so that it formed a dark grey wall over by the lane's end.

And turned to hail.

The air up ahead of him became filled with translucent rocks the size of cannonballs. They fell with such force, it sounded to Caleb like a hundred thousand drums began beating all at once. Trees shivered and wrenched and lost limbs. The militia trucks were flattened. Roofs in the distance were blasted open. Windows shattered.

Caleb had no idea how long the barrage continued. It

seemed to him like hours, but he doubted it was more than a few minutes. When it ended, the rain resumed its course, falling upon them in natural waves.

From their attackers there was no sign. No sound. Nothing. Even the alarms had gone silent.

Caleb turned to where Pablo and his crew watched from a roofline. He waved both arms and shouted, "We have to go!"

Pablo waved back, called to his others, and vanished.

Caleb turned and signaled to Kevin. His friend's wolfish grin was visible from where he and Dale stood by the city's boundary fence. Kevin said something, the slender young man lifted his arms high, and directly ahead of where they stood . . .

The city's boundary wall flattened to the earth.

The space was not more than twenty feet wide, little broader than the trucks. Kevin patted the younger man on the shoulder and ran back toward them.

Caleb yelled, "Everybody in the trucks!"

The first truck started and trundled forward. The second driver ground the gears terribly before lurching into line. Caleb had no idea who was behind the wheel, nor did he much care. Pablo and Kevin scrambled behind the wheel of the two militia trucks that had halted by the two they had stolen from the militia headquarters. Caleb helped pile the last remaining team and their family into the backs. The engines started, then Forrest yelled for Caleb to climb on board.

Pablo's truck became stuck with two wheels on the curb and two others mired in the sodden grass. Kevin jammed his vehicle into the back of Pablo's, shoving the truck across the rain-slick lawn and through the opening. Caleb was seated by the third truck's rear gate and felt the jarring bumps as they crossed the flattened brush. The youngest children from Maddie's group wailed a continuous note. He found he did not mind the noise. It formed a high-pitched testimony to the fact that they had survived thus far.

Once they were all through, they halted on the gravel road encircling the city's perimeter fence. Kevin leapt down and yelled for Caleb to join him. Together they raced back through the barrier to where Dale stood groaning under the strain. His entire body shook like a tuning fork.

Caleb shouted, "Help me lift him!"

Kevin gripped Dale's waist as Caleb took hold beneath the young man's outstretched arms. Together they hauled Dale through the aperture. They lowered him to the earth, and Caleb told Dale, "Let go!"

With a groaning rustle, the boundary fence folded back into place.

They were free.

They drove through most of the night, stopping occasionally for hurried discussions and even hastier bites from the sacks of stolen food. Each time, the six of them traded ideas. Kevin, Caleb, and Pablo were joined by Carla, Irene, and Maddie, everyone talking at once, and all of them so tired they neither took note of nor cared where the ideas originated. All the mentats who had not succumbed to exhaustion were ordered to send out waves of intent, telling anyone who sought them that they were headed south, south, south. Over and over the message rang out, as though the mentats were talking among themselves, which they were. Discussing what life would be like once they reached the southern boundary, passed Jacksonville, and entered the dead zone.

In truth, as soon as the trail they followed met a better road, they headed north.

Caleb only shared the barest of impressions with the others. But it was enough. None of them required a more careful explanation. Nor did they have time to deliberate. Their trust in him and his plan was that strong.

Near dawn, Forrest directed Kevin and the other drivers down a rutted trail that ended by a derelict farmhouse. The rain stopped just as the group halted. They arranged the vehicles in a semicircle around the barn, the only structure with half a roof. They hauled bedrolls and blankets inside, hunting down dry spots and scattering field mice in the process. Caleb waited while Pablo and Kevin set the guard roster, then threw himself down and was gone.

Sometime after daybreak Caleb dreamed of the eagle design. Only this time it was etched like empty branches against a wintry sky. He opened his eyes, fully awake now, his mind filled with impressions from the dream.

He rose from the bedroll he'd shared with a young boy no more than six or seven years of age. He took pen and paper from his pack and walked to the watch fire that burned in what was left of the farmhouse kitchen. A pail of water rested upon the stone-lined well. Caleb drank deep, washed his face, then seated himself upon a fallen roof beam.

He was busy writing when Maddie walked over and joined him. He did not need to look up to know it was her. Nor did she find any need to speak. Even now, as he hastily scribbled down everything he could recall from this latest event, he felt surrounded by the immensity of her love. It was like a great wave of emotion had approached with her, and now it enveloped him. Patiently waiting while he wrote.

When he set the notes aside, he looked up in time to see the eastern sky begin to clear. Brilliant streamers fell through the cloud covering, turning every surface into crystal prisms. He turned to face Maddie, and for the first time since the mad rush began, he studied her intently. Maddie continued to watch the fire, granting him space for a long and unhurried look.

There were subtle differences from the way Caleb remembered her. She was taller than he recalled, for one thing. And her hair seemed thicker, with more blonde shades amid the brown. Her hands were seamed and the nails rimmed by torn skin. She was also quieter now, or so it seemed to him. The silence was more than just an absence of words. She carried a new stillness at a bone-deep level. And she looked exhausted. Her eyes were framed by plum circles as dark as bruises. Her skin appeared translucent, as if her fatigue had stripped away an external layer.

They were surrounded by the soft patter of droplets falling from exposed rafters and the trees. Caleb could hear snores from inside the barn. Farther out were the soft footfalls of mentats on sentry.

The fire's warm glow created a haven for them as Maddie softly spoke. "I knew, Caleb. I knew you would come. It wasn't through some form of far-seeing. That's your gift. I knew because I know you. I was certain all it would take was one cry, one plea, and you would do what was needed and be there. For me. For all of us."

Caleb resisted the urge to reach out and embrace her. She needed this chance to speak, as he had to study her.

Maddie watched the crackling fire and went on, "I had no evidence, nothing I could show the others. We couldn't risk contacting you. I knew the suits had watchers in place. So late at night I shared with all those who could connect by thoughts or images or emotions . . ."

"We call them mentats," Caleb said.

She nodded acceptance. "I shared with our mentats what I knew about the man I love."

"How many mentats are there among you?"

"It's so hard to say. The youngest ones are . . . I suppose flexible is the best word to describe them. Most of them received enough to tell their families I was going to make everything okay. The adult mentats did the same." She looked at him, revealing the golden flecks in her gaze, the unshed tears. "It was so hard, Caleb. I've spent my entire life hiding. But here I was, using my secret gift to share the deepest part of what I knew about the man I love."

He reached for her then. She molded herself to him. They sat like that, warmed by far more than a meager fire, until approaching footsteps sounded behind them and Kevin asked, "Can we join you?"

"Yes," Caleb said, and straightened, because it was time.

They were joined by Carla and Irene and Pablo and Forrest. Then Dale and Tula and Hank. Tea was made in the water pail, the largest container they possessed, and gradually others came over and seated themselves.

While they shared what food they had left and passed around mugs, Caleb used a blank sheet of paper and drew the image he had now envisioned twice, that of the eagle in full flight. He handed it to Maddie, who passed it on. As it made the rounds, Caleb said, "I have a plan."

They entered Charlotte by the last light of a fading day. The sky was washed utterly clear. They were all exhausted by the journey. One of the trucks had been lost when its front axle broke. Another simply ran out of fuel. Those passengers had been redistributed. Now they were crammed in so tightly most of their packs had been jettisoned. There had been complaints, but not many, for even the youngest members understood the critical need for haste.

Caleb had divided their meager band into two teams. He had wanted to travel to Fort Mills and be there to take on Hollis. But Kevin and Pablo were insistent. He was their leader, and he needed to be seen as the one who conquered the mayor's palace. Caleb wanted to argue, for the step carried a sense of greater burdens to come. Then Maddie chimed in as well, and Caleb's protests had gone unspoken.

Barry had used his powers to stifle communication. How far he reached or how much he actually achieved, no one knew. But when they arrived at the city's southern gates, the militia was caught completely off guard. As were the sentries around the officers' residence compound and the main barracks and training grounds. Wherever the group stopped and directed their mental weapons, the militia scattered in full panic.

They halted at the outlying militia barracks long enough for a hot meal and fresh vehicles. Then one group drove to the militia headquarters, while Caleb and his team set off for the city's heart.

Maddie stood beside Caleb now as they drove through the gates that Dale had pried open. All the militia on duty around the mayor's palace had long since fled. The pristine garden fronting the palace itself was just as Kevin had described, a beautiful array of flowers watered by the sweat and tears of workers scarcely better off than slaves of old. Serfs, Kevin had called them, products of a regime that deserved its fate.

Caleb and his team climbed down from the truck and stood in front of the silent house. There was movement by the second-floor window, a quick jerk of a curtain, then nothing.

Forrest said, "I detect no guns."

"It's a shame," Dale said, "to destroy such a beautiful building."

"No it's not," Maddie replied.

Caleb took a long breath. It had never been about simply rescuing Maddie. In truth, he now viewed her imprisonment as a terrible necessity. Not just for himself but for the awakening of abilities and strengths among all his group. So that they could arrive here. And do what was required. So that they all might have a future.

The aim was far from simple, but as clear now as the sky overhead. They were to establish a new enclave. One standing upon the same principles of equality and democracy that had been put in place when their nation was first founded. Rule of law, Kevin had often repeated. Every citizen was to be treated equally, regardless of power or status or abilities. And all were to be made welcome.

Especially adepts.

Their days of running in fear were over.

Maddie said, "Caleb."

"Yes?"

"The others say they're ready."

He took a long breath, then said, "Attack."

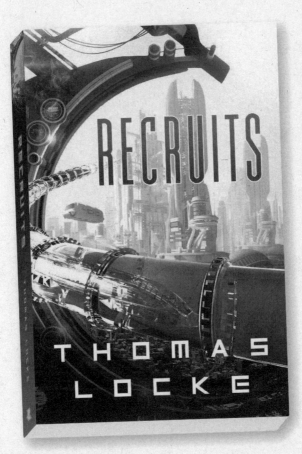

Ten years ago this month, they started drawing the train station, one positioned on another world.

They had the same image burning in their brains, in their *hearts*. The station was a tube pinched at both ends, like a twisted candy wrapper. They argued over how big it was. A couple of miles long at least. And the trains, they were all glass. Not like trains with windows. Glass trains. And the tubes they traveled in, glass as well. But that wasn't the best part.

The trains came and went all over the tube. Top, sides, bottom. Gravity modulation, that was definitely Dillon's term. Sean assumed his brother got the concept from some sci-fi novel, but Dillon insisted it came to him in a dream. Whatever. They drew the station on sheets from sketch pads and pasted them all over their two rooms. Walls and ceilings.

Forget posters of rock groups and models. Even as they entered their teens, there was nothing they wanted more than to build on the dream. Leave the same-old behind. And fly to a world they were somehow sure was more than just a figment of two imaginations. So they kept drawing, adding cities of lyrical majesty that rose beyond the station. They were connected to this place like the ticket was in the mail. Ten years had changed nothing.

The idea came to them when they were seven. Nowadays Dillon claimed it was his concept. But Sean knew his twin was just blowing smoke. Dillon had a highly convenient memory. He remembered things the way he wished they were. Sean decided it wasn't worth arguing over. Dillon tended to go ballistic whenever his remake of history was challenged. But Sean knew the idea was his. Totally.

Still, he let Dillon claim he was the one who came up with the concept. The one that powered them through the worst times. Kept them moving forward. That was the most important thing. They had it in their bones.

Only that spring, the concept and all the bitter yearnings attached to it actually did change into something more.

They were coming from the school bus, walking the line of cookie-cutter homes in suburban Raleigh. They lived in a development called Plantation Heights, six miles northeast of the old town, the cool town. All the good stuff was farther west. The Research Triangle Park. Duke University. UNC Chapel Hill. NC State. Five different party centrals. That particular Friday afternoon was great, weather-wise. Not too hot, nice breeze, Carolina blue sky. Two weekends before the end of the school year was also good for a high, even if they were both still looking for a job. Just two more of the local horde, searching for grunt work that paid minimum wage at best. But their eighteenth birthdays were only four months and six days off. That summer they would take their SATs and begin the process of trying to find a university that would accept them both. Because they definitely wanted to stay together. No matter how weird the world might find it, the topic had been cemented in a conversation that lasted, like, eleven seconds.

The biggest focus for their summer was to find something that paid enough to buy a car. Their rarely used drivers' licenses burned holes in their back pockets. Their desire to acquire wheels and escape beautiful suburbia fueled an almost daily hunt through the want ads.

Dillon looked up from his phone and announced, "Dodge is coming out with a new Charger SRX. Five hundred and seventy-one ponies."

Sean tossed his brother his backpack. "I'm not hauling your weight for you to go trolling for redneck clunkers."

Dillon stowed his phone and slung his pack. "You and your foreign junk."

"Seven-series BMW, V12, blow your Charger into last week."

"For the cost of a seven-series we could get two Chargers and take our ladies to New York for a month."

"The kind of ladies who would set foot in a Charger would rather go to Arkansas, buy some new teeth."

They turned the corner and saw a U-Haul partly blocking their drive. Two hefty guys were shifting furniture from the truck into the house next door. Moving trucks were a fairly common sight in Plantation Heights. The development held over three hundred houses. Or rather, one home cloned three hundred times. Which was how Sean came up with his name for the residences and the people who lived here. Clomes.

They stopped, mildly curious over who was moving in next door.

Dillon said, "For a moment there I thought maybe Big Phil had decided to relocate us."

"Fat chance."

"We're going to walk in and he'll tell us we're turning urban. We'll move into a downtown loft. Burn the polyester and go Armani."

Sean had a quip ready. He always did. Two o'clock in the morning, he'd be woken up by some comment his brother had dreamed up, literally. The response was always there, just waiting. Only this time his retort died unspoken, because their new neighbor came out his front door.

Adult clomes basically came in two shapes. The fitness freaks had skinny moms and overpumped dads. They talked about their bikes or their yoga or their weekend trips to hike around Maui in an hour. The other clomes wore their sofas like lounge suits. The farthest they moved was to the fridge or the backyard grill. They talked about . . . Actually, Sean didn't really care what they talked about.

Their new neighbor definitely did not fit in Clome Heights.

For one thing, he only had one hand.

The left sleeve of his shirt was clipped up, hiding the stump that ended just below his elbow. He limped as he walked. He was lean and dark complexioned, like he'd been blasted by some foreign sun for so long his skin was permanently stained. This man could have taken the biggest guy in

Plantation Heights and turned him into a clome sandwich. One-handed.

When the guy turned around, they probably saw the scar at the same moment, because Dillon dragged in the breath Sean had trouble finding. The scar emerged from the top of his shirt, ran around the left side of his neck, clipped off the bottom third of his ear, and vanished into his hairline. Military-style crew cut. Of course. The jagged wound was punctuated with scar tissue the size and shape of small flowers.

Their neighbor spoke to the two movers in a language that didn't actually sound like he was talking. More like he *sang* the words. And they responded the same way. How three big guys could sing and sound tough at the same time, Sean had no idea. But they did.

Then they saluted. Like Roman soldiers in the old movies. Fist to chest. Another little chant. Then the movers got in the U-Haul and drove away.

The guy then turned and stared at them. Which was when Sean realized there was something mildly weird about two teenage kids standing in the street, gawking at this guy like they were looking through a cage at the zoo. For once, Sean's nimble mind came up with nada. He just stood there. The intensity of that man's look froze Sean's brain.

Their neighbor said, "So. You must be the twins. Kirrel, correct?" He waved his good hand at the front door. "Want to come inside for a cup of tea?"

Dillon managed, "Uh, we've got homework."

The guy seemed to find that mildly humorous. "That is the best excuse you can manage?"

Sean probably would have stood there all night if his

brother had not snagged his arm and pulled him away. "Have a nice day," he said.

Dillon waited until they were inside to say, "'Have a nice day'? Really?"

"Go start your homework, why don't you." Sean moved to the front window. But the guy was gone. The street was empty. Silent. Just another day in Clomeville. Except for the man who had just moved in next door.

Thomas Locke is a pseudonym for **Davis Bunn,** an award-winning novelist with worldwide sales of seven million copies in twenty-five languages. Davis divides his time between Oxford and Florida and holds a lifelong passion for speculative stories. He is the author of the Legends of the Realm, Fault Lines, and Recruits series. Learn more at www.tlocke.com.

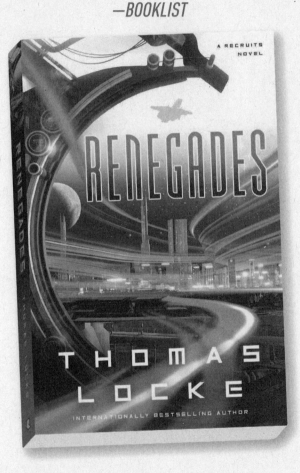

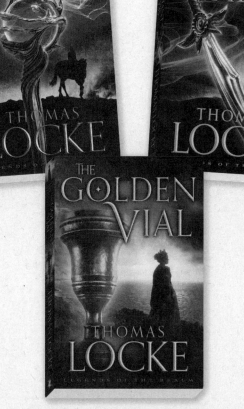

What if reality is only the

EDGE OF POSSIBILITY?

Psychological thrillers from Thomas Locke!